THE CANDIDATE'S MAID
Part One

A Spy in Stilettos

THE CANDIDATE'S MAID
Part One

A Spy in Stilettos

LAURA LIS SCOTT

Toot Sweet Ink

tootsweet.ink

Boulder

Cover and interior design copyright ©2016 Toot Sweet Inc.
All rights reserved.

A Toot Sweet Ink Book
Published by Toot Sweet Inc.
6525 Gunpark Drive Suite 370
Boulder, CO 80301

Visit us at tootsweet.ink

Toot Sweet Ink is a trademark of Toot Sweet Inc.

Library of Congress Control Number:
First Edition

ISBN: 978-1-943194-10-0 (hardback)
ISBN: 978-1-943194-08-7 (trade paper)
ISBN: 978-1-943194-09-4 (ePub)

To Mom,
who has always believed

THE CANDIDATE'S MAID
Part One

Contents

THE CANDIDATE'S MAID
Part One

A Spy in Stilettos

1

I SUPPOSE *I* SHOULD TELL you how I ended up here, in a Hudson River Valley mansion's sumptuous marble bathroom at ten thirty at night, dressed like a wet dream in a little black silk dress, four-inch Manolos, and yellow rubber gloves, standing over a massive bald man wearing a charcoal Westmancott suit and chunks of supper, who was passed out on the marble floor.

This was not the job for which I had applied fifteen hours earlier. No. This was not a job for a PhD, even a hitherto unemployed one. Then again, maybe I wasn't quite in the position to be picky. I really needed the money. A lot of money. And I couldn't just leave Mr. Henderson passed out there on the floor. The Colonel, my new employer, was counting on me.

So how was I going to get him cleaned up and into his waiting Bentley—all without any of the other guests made the wiser?

I broke down the problem: Mr. Henderson was pretty much out of it. He was now thoroughly bevomited. And he was big.

Football-player big. Twenty-five-years-later-without-workouts-football-player big. There was no way I was going to be able to drag him out to the car. And since I had to be discreet, getting help was out of the question.

Hmmm . . .

I came up with a plan: Clean him up. Roll him over, if I could. And then somehow get him to the garden exit. I took hold of his wrist and pulled. And pulled. And pulled. And paused to catch my breath. He was not budging. It was like he was glued to the floor. Maybe the Colonel had a forklift handy.

Okay, that wasn't such a good plan. No, I would have to get him up under his own power at least enough for him to walk all the way to the garden entrance.

I set to work: I dropped a couple of towels onto the floor, stepped onto them in my stilettos, shuffle-stepped a bit to coax the chunky liquid into a puddle to the side, and stepped off, leaving the towels as temporary dams. So far so good.

Facedown in a puddle, Mr. Henderson snortled and sighed. Was he awake?

"Mr. Henderson?"

No response. And the fruity aroma wasn't dissipating. I had to escape into the hallway, gasping for a little fresh air to settle my own dry heaves. I couldn't allow myself to add to the problem. After a few deep lungfuls, I held my breath and charged back in.

Mr. Henderson had rolled himself to his side and was now semiconscious. I wetted a fresh towel and carefully wiped his ruddy face and neck. I tried brushing the worst off of his shirt.

"Ah . . . good . . ." he slurred. "Detton's death is a blessing . . . so we can use this to . . ."

Detton again. They were talking about him all night. Three days before, famous television minister and senatorial candidate Pip Detton had been found dead in a Baltimore hotel room. The headlines shouted: "Detton Dead and Dominated"; "Pip Pacified by Prince"; "Detton Found Dead—You Won't Believe What They Found!" Apparently he had expired while strapped down to a bed, with a binky in his mouth, a dog collar around his neck, and a Prince Albert piercing around . . . where *it* goes. (That last part wasn't mentioned in the *fit to print* papers. Editorial standards, you know?)

Mr. Henderson coughed. "Arrhhg . . ." he said, ". . . perfect timing . . ."

Perfect timing for death? I hoped he was just babbling.

He snuffled a bit and looked around. "What am I doing down here?"

"Mr. Henderson, how are you? Do you think you can stand?"

His eyes focused on me. "Oh," he said. "Hey, sweetheart." With sudden energy, he propped himself up on an elbow and frowned at me. "Lemme ask you . . . question." He closed his eyes and swallowed, then gave me a bleary look. "Are you political?"

"Political?" I asked.

"D'you follow politics?"

"I vote, if that's what you mean." I wasn't going to elaborate— let alone admit to my father's career. No point with a drunk.

"Would you rather vote for"—he took a breath—"an extremist, hypocritical, perverted son of a bitch or an upstand-ing"—another breath—"dignified man of breeding?"

"Does either of them tell the truth?"

He snorted. Chuckled. And then started laughing. "I like you, sweetheart."

It was time to get him moving. "Can you do me a favor, Mr. Henderson? Can you stand up?"

"When?"

"How about now?"

"Oh . . . Let's . . . find out." He just lay there for a few seconds, grunted, then started heaving himself up, and got as far as his hands and knees. "I think I made a bit of a mess."

"It's nothing, Mr. Henderson," I said. "Let's keep going. You're doing great." Grasping the counter, he got one foot up under him. "Careful now," I cautioned, "the floor's a bit slippery."

In one smooth motion, he was up—a bit unsteady, but standing. He really was tall. Even in the spike-heeled pumps they had me wear, I came up only to his nose.

It took three more towels to get the worst of the mess off of his trousers, but everything was still too wet. My eyes zeroed in on the toilet paper, which kind of did the trick, although the wool was left covered in tiny bits of paper lint.

"Miss Baker," said a woman's voice behind me. Ms. Vitiello, a slender, dark Italian New Yorker from Sheepshead Bay, and the only other maid approximating my age, had one hand covering her nose, the other holding up Mr. Henderson's overcoat—a godsend! Now I could wrap him up in something clean.

"Thank you!" I gushed, grabbing the coat quickly while keeping a steadying hand on Mr. Henderson's back. "Garden exit! Where is it?"

With her chin, Ms. Vitiello gestured down the corridor. "Down the promenade. Go straight all the way. Can't miss it."

"Thanks!"

She glanced up at the teetering-but-upright Mr. Henderson, gave me a raised eyebrow, turned on her heel, and clacked away, still covering her nose.

It took some work to get his coat onto him because he kept trying to help, getting his arm in the wrong sleeve, turning the wrong way, but finally I had him bundled and ready for delivery.

I peered right into his eyes, trying to see him in there. "Are you ready to walk?"

He smiled. "You have the most beautiful eyes." He dropped his head, exhausted. "Why do they always have such beautiful eyes?" The charms of drunken men.

His arm was too big for my hands to get around, so I wrapped my arm through his. "Mr. Henderson, we're going to take a step now."

"A step?"

"Move your foot."

He leaned to one side and lifted his foot . . . and clomped forward. We were moving. I guided him out into the hall.

As we made our way down the corridor, he managed a slow but steady tottering pace—accompanied by more half-coherent rambling, which I did my best to tune out. I had to focus on keeping him balanced, alternating between serving as a cane under his weight and a counterbalance preventing him from tipping away.

"We can do this," he said. Silly me, I thought he was talking about making it to his car. But then he continued, ". . . now that Detton's out of the picture."

Curious, I tried to draw him out. "Yes?"

But he just huffed and grunted from the effort of walking.

Snow was still falling steadily outside. The midnight air felt cool and refreshing. I sucked in several deep breaths.

A long black Bentley limousine stood idling, headlights burning. The chauffeur—a wan old relic in cap and livery—jumped out of the driver's seat and trotted around. He was as diminutive as Mr. Henderson was ginormous. With gloved hands, he opened the rear door.

Inside sat Mrs. Henderson, wrapped in matronly furs, looking rather peeved, poor woman. *How often has she had to deal with this?*

The chauffeur came over and took Mr. Henderson's other arm, and we both led him slowly across the ice-packed pavement to the car.

"Watch your head," the chauffeur bleated.

Slowly at first, and then more quickly as gravity took over, Mr. Henderson flopped into the seat. In very businesslike fashion, the chauffeur picked up his employer's weighty feet and shoved them into the car. Mr. Henderson stirred. "Hey." His half-closed eyes found me. "What's your name?"

I smiled at him. A momentary impulse to rebel urged me to say, *Dr. Melody Baker*—in his state, he'd never remember. But I was good. I said simply, "Miss Baker."

He said, "Huh."

The chauffeur closed the door, gave me a grim nod, and hobbled—much more slowly now—back to the driver's side. A moment later, the Bentley pulled away into the darkness, tires crackling on the ice.

That was done. Success!

I took one step back toward the mansion—my heel skated out—and suddenly I was on my side.

First I was stunned—then outraged that the ground dared do this to me. My knee throbbed. My neck ached. My head was ringing. Tears froze on my face. I wanted to just lie there, but a steady cold breeze drove a chill into my bones.

"Shit!"

2

EIGHTEEN HOURS EARLIER, I was sitting in the quiet of Café Proteus, my local haunt in East Harlem, working on my third refill of dark roast, and staring at my computer and the unavoidable reality that my rent was four months past due, my student loans were crashing down, and—despite having spent a year bent over *The Chronicle of Higher Education*'s job listings and sending one hundred and thirty-two applications into the academic void—I had not gotten a single interview, even by phone.

It didn't help knowing that I had made myself some kind of academic Typhoid Mary when I had decided on the topic of my dissertation: "Deconstructing Deconstruction: The Rhetoric of Postmodernism and the Demise of Critical Thinking"—which sounds impressive, sure, but so far had not impressed any English departments anywhere. If my academic advisor at Columbia had warned me that I would emerge from my 246-thousand-dollar, student-loan-financed education regarded as an academic blasphemer, maybe I would have picked a safer topic, like "The Existentialism of Lady Gaga" or "The Shakespearean Tradition in Reality TV." I don't know. I think Professor Markley was amused by my hubris.

So now my only job prospects comprised serving drinks at Skoochy's Cabaret in Midtown or serving carnal pleasures as a girlfriend-for-hire.

I needed options.

I refreshed the jobs page, and a new listing gave me hope:

Immediate Opening: Full-time Research Assistant
Must be smart, organized, presentable, resourceful self-starter who needs little supervision and embodies grace under pressure.

• Strong writing skills. Graduate degree a plus.
• Compensation: commensurate with ability.

Perfect! Research I could do. I had a kick-ass graduate degree. I was more than ready to work full-time. And here I was, with my financial world crumbling all around me. *Grace under pressure* described me to a tee. But the last line of the listing killed me:

• Location: Hudson River Valley, outside of Cold Spring.

Crap.

I sat there, alternating between staring at that listing and staring out the window. I did not want to leave New York City—not a chance, not to work a day job.

And Cold Spring, where the hell was that? I looked it up. Way the fuck out of town, up in the wilderness, where people get bitten by deer ticks, horseflies, vampire bats, black widow spiders, and rattlesnakes! I was quite certain the roads wouldn't be paved and cafés would be scarce. And there was no way I'd be able to buy oranges at three a.m.

It would be life in the sticks. Or an epic nightmare of a commute from the city.

But: *Graduate degree a plus.*

And I needed to do *something*.

But with my checking account running on vapors and only forty-three bucks in my purse, I wasn't likely to be buying much of anything anywhere at three a.m., or any other time.

I emailed them my CV and refilled my coffee.

Twenty minutes later, I received a reply:

> **Excellent qualifications. Are you able to come in today for an interview?**

I blinked. Right there on my screen was the first interview request I had received since graduating. I couldn't believe it. For a solid minute, I read and re-read the email, daring it to change into the typical rejection. But it didn't change.

I jumped out of my chair and shattered the peaceful quiet of the café. "Yes!"

3

OR THE FIRST TIME in four years, I stood before my mirror in my navy Tahari suit, which never would have fit had I not been subsisting for the past three months on a daily diet of one hard-boiled egg, one-half can of white tuna, and coffee—lots of coffee. You see, I've always been on the large side. My mom would always say I was just a *big girl*. That was me. Big girl. (In middle school in California, it was pretty much unbearable to be around the other girls with their petite bodies and dainty hands and cute little feet. The still-shrimpy boys, who scarcely came up to my shoulders, would call me *Blondezilla* and roar like monsters before dashing away, giggling. Annoying little fucks. That ended when we moved to DC and my breasts started growing. Then the boys named me *Boobzilla*. High school, the fount of maturity.)

In the context of my usual, sensible big-girl-in-the-big-city fashion line of sweats, jeans, sneakers, and concert T-shirts, the suit gave me a feeling of being a real professional, even if managing *grace under pressure* in the one-and-a-half-inch heels of my matching navy Mootsies Tootsies pumps would possibly present a challenge.

Someone knocked on my door, but time was short—only forty-five minutes to catch my train—so I ignored it and brushed out my hair into something more presentable than a rat's nest and set to applying some make-up. After quickly inserting my good-luck pilcrow earrings (because what marks a new paragraph in life more than getting a new job?), I made one last mirror check.

I was dressed for interviewing success.

When I stepped out of my apartment, I saw tacked to my door a document:

WRITTEN DEMAND FOR PAYMENT OF PAST-DUE RENT

I had three days to pay up or move out. It listed the thousands of dollars I was in arrears.

Fuck fuck fuck! I know how much I owe!

I decided I had to deal with this later. I couldn't miss my train. Besides, wouldn't getting a job be dealing with it?

Forty minutes later, the dazzling sunlight shining through the windows into Grand Central Station stopped me in my tracks. It felt like a cathedral, except with no pews and the four-sided clock serving as altar. Footsteps and voices of the bustling travelers echoed in the hall. For a few moments I just stood there, picturing myself among the commuters, marching with purpose to and from work.

A clean-shaven, raw-boned man with pitted pink cheeks and a rumpled plaid jacket appeared in front of me, standing too close and smelling vaguely of bleu cheese. In a crackly voice, he recited as if by rote, "Please, can you help me, I was robbed, they took my wallet, I don't have enough money to get back home."

My automatic city response kicked in and I stepped away, muttering, "Sorry."

"Fucking cunt bitch!" he snapped at my back. Did I tell you that's another one of my names? You can collect quite a few on the streets of New York. (Some of my other favorites are Yo Lady Suck My Dick, Hey Babe Come To My Place And I'll Open New Worlds To You, Fuck You White Whore, and You Know You Want It. It's all quite creative, don't you think? Maybe I should collect them all in a baby names book and donate the profits to a women's shelter.)

Getting on the train actually felt something like reaching sanctuary. I found an empty seat, hunkered down against the window, and put on my public-transportation grimace to deter people from sitting next to me. It worked for a few minutes.

Facing this trip into the unknown, I had to tell Petra. I pulled out my phone and texted:

Going upstate for a job interview.

Petra was my one best friend. Unlike me, she had her shit together. She knew who she was, what she wanted, and how to get it.

Petra was pretty, with dark hair, dark eyes, and a dark aura that gave her a gothic aspect without even trying, which stood her in good stead in the city; yet it was her easy bearing, like she was the center of the universe, that struck me the first time I met her back when I moved into the university apartment she and I shared. I was new to the city and found it to be alien, noisy, aggressive, and exciting. By contrast, she, who had been in America only two months, seemed to be in her native element. Uptown, downtown, noisy street, Central Park, fancy restaurant, Katz Deli, it didn't matter—she always fit right in like she was born to be there. I was the dorky blonde girl who didn't fit in anywhere, so she was my pass into the world.

Maybe it was her Eastern European upbringing, but to her everything—*everything*—had an obvious truth to it or was not worth considering; and when she was questioned on it, a shrug sufficed as answer enough. "The President is focused on building empire." Shrug. "Pluto is either planet or not planet." Shrug. "Only women know how to please women." Shrug.

"It's not as simple as that," I'd reply. And she'd shrug again. For me, everything had nuance. Nothing was cut and dried. Even facts had asterisks—qualifications to contextualize the limits of what was known.

"You always ask, 'How true is true?'" she said to me once. "Why is this?"

I shrugged, which from me meant, *I don't know.*

Through the window of the train, I watched the people on the platform, picking out the New Yorkers from the out-of-towners. The latter wore white sneakers and puffy jackets in fruit colors; the former tended to wear wool coats or leather jackets, power shoes (oxfords, boots, or vampy heels), and lots of black overall—black being the uniform for the city since the days of coal.

My phone clicked. Petra had replied:

> *college?*

> No. A day job. I need to pay rent.

upstate???

It's a long shot.

hope good $

I'm at the point where *any* money is good money.

gl

Thanks.

With a gentle nudge, the platform started sliding forward and I realized I was sitting in a backward-facing seat. Who the hell came up with backward-facing seats? Does anybody actually *enjoy* sitting backwards on a train? I certainly don't. It made me sick—a sad fact I'd learned years ago in the very back of my mother's ancient Buick Estate Wagon—*the boat*, as we called it. I glanced around the train car, looking for an open seat facing the other way, but they were all at least half-occupied, and just then I didn't relish sharing a seat with an unknown person with unknown hygiene, unknown chattiness, or unknown manners.

My phone clicked. Petra again.

nester cming. Epic

Nester? I didn't know who that was, or why she'd be so excited about him, but asking her was preempted by the unceremonious flopping into the seat next to me of a short, round, bald man with a fat flap-top briefcase and a face dripping with sweat. He smelled like garlic, rum, and peppermint.

I folded my arms and curled myself up as small as I could against the window. He didn't get off until the stop before mine. At least he didn't hit on me.

4

After a half hour on a two-lane highway winding up into forested hills, tires squealing on the switchbacks, and another ten minutes sliding around on an unpaved road, the cab stopped at a giant wrought-iron gate decorated with some kind of coat of arms—two stars and a bar over a lion. High stone walls with pikes on top flanked the entrance, extending out as far as I could see, disappearing in the dense pines. Apparently I was interviewing with a feudal baron prepared to defend against the barbarian horde.

Behind the gate, a man bundled in a black overcoat, standing still as a statue, watched us with gray eyes. I rolled down my window.

"Hi," I said.

He stared at me in silence.

"I'm Melody Baker. I'm here about a job?" He did not move, but suddenly the gate lurched into motion, swinging wide.

"Thanks," I said.

The man just swung his gaze up the road and back to me—which was apparently all I was going to get from him.

"Thanks. Nice talking to you," I said.

As the cab drove on, he pulled a gloved hand out of his pocket, brought it up next to his cheek, and spoke into his sleeve.

The driveway threaded uphill for another mile through thick stands of trees. At one point I caught a glimpse of the reddish façade of a four-story building. It seemed to be close, but we drove another five minutes before the road brought us to a large, sweeping plaza in front of it. It was a giant castle.

Yes, a castle.

No mere mansion, this was the kind of place where James Bond parks his Aston Martin next to the Ferraris, Maseratis, and Bugattis, strides in, drinks martinis, and plays Baccarat. This was the kind of place where the Queen of England would stay if she wanted to get away from it all and escape into the middle of nowhere.

The cab fare to get me to this nowhere exceeded my weekly grocery budget. I crossed my fingers and shoved my Visa into the card reader. A moment later, the transaction was approved. The cabbie gave me a business card. "Gimme at least an hour notice," she said. I got out and she gunned it, kicking rubble back against my ankles.

The building was a hundred yards wide—a massive gothic affair with rust-gray stone, paned windows, and battlements on the roof for the archers. The satellite dishes and fifty-foot ham radio antenna somehow made the building look older. I crunched across the gravel-strewn limestone to the marble portico steps and climbed up to the grandly carved double doors.

Before I could knock, the door opened slowly and a gentleman of middle years with trim brown hair and beard, dressed in a black morning coat, waistcoat, and pin-striped slacks, peered at me with a distant, inquisitive expression. The butler? He said nothing. I fought down a sudden flash of panic that I had come to the wrong house.

"I called this morning about the research assistant position?" That didn't sound at all as confident as I'd intended. "I have an appointment at two thirty?"

His brown eyes flitted over my appearance, down and up, and he sighed ever so slightly.

"Baker, Melody," he said in a gentle baritone as quiet as a whisper.

"Melody Baker, yes."

"Please come in." He moved aside, swinging the door wider.

I stepped across the threshold.

5

THE FOYER ALONE WAS bigger than my entire apartment—
not that that was saying much. My couch would've
been right there where the mahogany table stood with that vase
of two dozen flowers; my kitchenette, about thirty feet shy of
the French doors toward the back; my bed, just at the foot of
the stairs. The bright, circular skylight fifty feet overhead would
have added some cheer to my bedroom, but here it only lent
the space an austere and rather lonely aura.

The butler led me across the marble floor. Everything about
him conveyed grace and discipline: silent and smooth stride,
glassy black shoes, razor-creased slacks, trim jacket, perfectly
symmetrical collar, tight curls without a hair out of place . . .
Who's that meticulous? Who's that polished?

I clomped behind, trying not to limp from the very real blis-
ter forming on my heel.

We stopped at a set of ornately decorated, antique white, very
tall double doors.

He glanced at me—perhaps to see if I was ready—and said, "The Colonel will see you now," and pushed both of the doors open, revealing a gigantic, gorgeous library.

It gave the impression of an intellectual gymnasium. Dark mahogany bookcases filled with books lined the walls all around, framing several paned-glass windows, and continuing up, past a circumferential mezzanine, all the way to an ornate ceiling with suspended tiered chandeliers. Luscious red Persian carpets covered the floor. Clusters of antique tables and chairs decorated the space here and there.

Because the butler had said *the Colonel*, I half expected to meet a man in uniform with a bird emblazoned on his hat. Instead, a slender man of about sixty or so, with graying brown hair, wearing a burgundy jacket and open-collar shirt, stood in the center of the room, regarding me with curiosity.

The butler bowed and quietly announced, "Miss Baker, sir." I cringed at the *Miss* part, but refrained from correcting him. This was an interview. I wanted to be pleasant.

"Thank you, Haynes," the man said. "Miss Baker, please do come in."

As I entered the room, the doors closed gently behind me.

"Have a seat," he said, tapping two fingers on an antique Georgian armchair, and walked back around a long library table that he apparently used as a desk.

Under his gaze, I walked to the chair and sat—or, rather, perched on the edge of the seat, resisting a sudden onset of performance anxiety that the seven cups of coffee that morning had done nothing to ameliorate.

And I had to pee.

He sat in a thick red leather office chair and, for a good half minute, watched me with pale blue eyes, saying nothing, and I started to feel really small. It felt like forever. Was he waiting for me to speak? He had this almost imposing presence—handsome in a distinguished patriarch kind of way; yet the impression was more in how he carried himself, as if he were anchored in the universe, while I was flotsam that had simply blown in and landed on this chair. What is it about powerful people that does this to us? Intimidates us even without trying—especially when we desperately need a job? He seemed kind and gentlemanly so far, so why was my heart racing?

A ladybug crawled out from my sleeve and onto my hand. *Where did that come from? It's a sign! I'm going to be lucky*, I told myself, not believing it, but hey, I took what I could get. The red insect took flight and disappeared in the glare of the window.

"So, Miss Baker," he said finally.

I tried to give him my sweet, adorable smile, but I could feel that my face wasn't cooperating and it probably came out more like a grimace. My mouth was suddenly very, very dry. "It's Dr. Baker," I rasped.

"Of course. Apologies," he said. "You came all the way up from the city?"

I swallowed a mouthful of dry. "Yes, I did. I appreciate your taking the time to see me on such short notice, Mr. . . . ?"

"Please just address me as 'Colonel.' Everybody does." He smiled as if amused.

". . . Okay. Mr. Colonel."

"Just Colonel."

"Colonel."

He smiled like I had just learned a new math formula. "You must have had a bit of an arduous journey coming up here."

Arduous? I think I unconsciously smoothed my hair into place. Looking down, I noticed a splash of mud on my skirt. I still don't know how that got there.

"Would you care to join me for some tea?" the Colonel asked. He glanced to my left . . .

. . . where Haynes was holding a silver tray at my elbow. How did he get there without my noticing?

At that point I made a major blunder: I accepted the tea.

Interviewing 101, Item 17: *Never accept a cup and saucer during an interview, lest your nerves (already jangled by seven dark-roast coffees) betray you with shaking hands rattling the china.* (This appears between 16, *Don't put your feet up on the desk*, and 18, *Make sure you've tweezed your nose hairs.*)

I smiled at Haynes—"Thanks"—and tried to gracefully lift the teacup and saucer. They clattered against each other in my unsteady hands. But I wanted to be polite, so I ventured a thirsty sip—

"You must have taken the train. How long does that take these days?" the Colonel asked.

—and I slurped too much, scalding my mouth. I could just picture my tongue blistering like ham in a broiler. "Uhh—uhbahd oo ahrs," I managed to say, and moved to set the tea down—but now Haynes and the tray were gone.

I clattered the cup onto the saucer and held them with both hands over my lap, all the while trying to subtly suck in air to cool my tongue without his noticing. This interview was already a disaster, and it hadn't even started yet.

"The Hudson River Valley is beautiful this time of year," the Colonel said.

It is? I hadn't noticed. During the entire train ride up, I had stared at my uncertain future, as defined by a deep, jagged gouge someone had carved into the seat-back in front of me.

"I do appreciate your taking the time."

"Mah bleasure." My mouth felt like it was blistering.

Time to take the initiative!

With a bold flourish, I set the tea on the edge of his desk and dug into what had been my favorite and very fine Coach bag— my gift to myself when I'd passed my dissertation defense, but which now, in this place, felt somewhat plebeian—and pulled out my crisp manila envelope. "I brought a copy of my vita."

The Colonel laughed pleasantly and said, "We printed out what you sent to us." Some excitement crept into his voice. "We posted the position only this morning, and ten minutes later, there you were! It's nice to see such enthusiasm."

I stared at the slight smirk on his face. I had no words. Was he praising me or mocking me?

"To be honest," he continued, "you're our first applicant and, well, that was exciting for us, so we did some checking up on you."

He picked a thick binder up off the desk. What was he holding? *A dossier? What could be in there?* Some online profiles? I wasn't that much of a social media butterfly. The only potentially embarrassing things I had were some tattoo photos I had pinned—my way of enjoying ink without the commitment. *Maybe I should take those down.* But this binder was at least three inches thick.

Who was this guy? Did he have connections in the NSA? I was sensing that coming here was a big mistake. A drop of cold sweat rolled down my back.

He rose and approached me around the desk. "This is some original thinking," he said, and handed me the binder.

On the cover, it said:

DECONSTRUCTING DECONSTRUCTION: THE RHETORIC OF POSTMODERNISM AND THE DEMISE OF CRITICAL THINKING

My heart stopped. "How did you get my dissertation?"

"It *is* online." He chuckled, a bit too pleased with himself. "We're not complete fools, Miss Baker. It's quite a fascinating read."

"You read it? When?" Was he on an academic committee at one of the gazillion university departments to which I had applied?

Apparently *no*. "I read it this morning over breakfast," he said.

"I don't think so," I said, and pointedly hefted the binder. "My dissertation is over 120 thousand words."

"People must say you're quite uncharitable to Jacques Derrida and Paul de Man. I can see why you've had such difficulty in finding an academic position—especially after you essentially poked them all in the eye and called them hypocrites." His eyes almost twinkled.

Now he *was* mocking me. I was not amused. "What makes you think I've had difficulty?"

He tipped his head as if to say, *Isn't it obvious?* "Well, you're *here*, aren't you?"

I wanted to sag back into my chair.

"Not that working with me would be so terrible," he said.

"But I'm a realist. I apprehend that compared with university teaching positions, doing research for a billionaire—even an amiable billionaire such as myself—ranks quite a way down the list."

"I'm just looking for work," I said. "Interesting work," I added—just so he knew that I was actually interested in *this* job that was way down the list.

"Yes, it's that kind of economy, I'm afraid. Since the time you applied this morning, we've had seventeen other applicants and eleven of those also have PhDs."

But I'm here first! I asked, "What field of research is this position for?"

"I'm afraid it's more in the area of politics. Not really something for a literature scholar."

It sounded like he was blowing me off. I couldn't let him do that. "I can do political science research," I said. "Research skills apply across fields."

"I'm sure that's true," he said. "Still, we're looking for a bit more expert knowledge of the ins and outs of politics. Someone who has things at his fingertips."

His fingertips? "But I do have expert knowledge." I didn't want to do what I was about to do—I wanted to make my way on my own, without help—but I was desperate. "I grew up with politics," I said confidently.

His eyebrows shot up. I had his interest. "What, one of your parents was in the PTA?"

"Congress."

"Really?" He looked up and pressed his lips together. "Baker. Baker. Not Max Baker, the California rep who filibustered that bill to rename the Grand Canyon the Ronald Reagan Freedom Canyon? That Baker?"

"That's the one," I said with a sinking feeling of disappointment in myself. If I got this job, it would be at least in part because of my connection to my father, who would just love to needle me about it.

The Colonel said, "So, you're a Congress brat."

"Since elementary school."

"That's good to know, Miss Baker."

"Dr. Baker."

He slammed closed his eyes. "Of course. Apologies." He placed his palms down on the table and looked at me. "Anything else?"

"Do I have the job?"

"I couldn't say. As I said, you're our first applicant. We have more resumés to review, and I have other matters to attend. I expect I'll be able to make a decision in a week or two."

A week or two? I'd be homeless by then! I couldn't let this opportunity go. "The ad was for an immediate opening. I'm ready to go immediately."

"And that's a point in your favor. Now, if there's not anything else—"

On the far wall, a section of bookcase swung out, revealing a dimly lit passageway from which emerged Haynes. Secret hidden doors. *So that's how Haynes sneaks around.* He glided quickly over to the Colonel and bent close. I could make out only a few words. ". . . Ohio cancelled . . . nobody . . . feed her goats . . ."

The Colonel's joviality slipped away to be replaced by gravitas. "I take it that leaves us short for tonight."

Haynes nodded. "Yes, sir. Short-staffed in general."

"What I really care about is tonight. Who else can we get?"

"I've been inquiring all week at our usual places, sir. They have nobody before late next week."

"What about old Yarrow? Perhaps he can lend us Johnson or that new girl of his . . ."

"Miss Emberevo."

"Emberevo, right."

"Unfortunately, Mr. Yarrow's staff is unavailable, sir, as they are engaged this evening."

"That's right, it's his bridge night," the Colonel said.

"Dungeons and Dragons, sir."

The Colonel straightened in his chair. "Well, keep looking, Haynes. If we have to send the jet and fly a promising student out from Denver—"

"I'm afraid it's too late for that, sir," Haynes said.

"That's unacceptable, Haynes."

"Sir, the guests start arriving in less than two hours."

The Colonel's face soured into a scowl.

And that's when I had my brilliant idea.

6

I CAN DO IT," I said.

  They looked at me.

"Do what?" the Colonel asked, truly puzzled.

"I can fill in," I said, exuding as much can-do spirit as I could muster. "I can be your staffer."

The Colonel shook his head. "Miss Baker, the position we're discussing is a maid, not a research assistant."

A maid? I knew nothing about maiding. But I couldn't back down now. I needed a job—any job. Sure, I could be a maid. "I understand. I can be your maid tonight. It's just cleaning rooms and making up some beds, right?"

The Colonel said, "Haynes, maybe you could clarify for Dr. Baker"—and he paused, perhaps enjoying the irony—"the nature of what being a maid means here in this house."

Haynes looked at me. "The position we're discussing is parlor maid or, more accurately, footman."

"Or in a lady's case," the Colonel said, "footwoman."

"Yes," said Haynes.

"But footwoman sounds rather ridiculous, doesn't it?" The Colonel laughed at his own joke.

Haynes didn't laugh. "This position entails providing professional, dignified, and elegant food and drink service for guests."

"Waiting tables? I've done that," I said with confidence. Hey, how different could parlor maiding be? "I can do this."

Haynes asked, "Have you ever been employed as a maid?"

"No, but I can learn."

He blew out an exhale of restrained exasperation. "Where did you wait tables?"

"Nice restaurants," I said defensively, but now I had to name them. I racked my brain. "Black Squirrel in DC and The Feed Bucket in New York. Square Dots Ice Creamery in Laguna, but that doesn't count." They didn't look impressed. *Come on, Mel!* "I've done catering." Nope, that wasn't doing it. "I worked the White House Correspondent's Dinner." *That* had their interest. "Twice!"

The Colonel asked, "How did you get that gig?"

I smiled. "Easier to get vetted if you're a Congressman's daughter."

Eyebrows raised, the Colonel looked from me to Haynes, who offered the slightest of shrugs.

I couldn't let this go now, so I did what I always do when I'm cornered and desperate: I told the truth. "Look," I said, "you're right, I've never worked as a maid, but you're in need, and I'm here, and I need work, and I think I can do this. Let me give it a try."

The Colonel grinned at this. "I like your spirit, Miss Baker."

This time, I smiled when I said, "Dr. Baker."

The Colonel and Haynes exchanged a look I couldn't read. The Colonel nodded. "All right, you have a deal."

Relief washed over me. But I'm not one to pass up opportunity. I saw my opening. "With a stipulation," I said.

The Colonel's face fell. With wary eyes, Haynes lifted his chin. They were on guard.

I continued, "I get the research assistant position once you find a new maid."

"Once we find . . ." The Colonel rubbed his chin. "You have a deal, Miss Baker."

"Dr. Baker."

He leaned back in his chair. "I keep my staff all on a last-name basis, Baker. Isn't that right, Haynes?"

"It is indeed, sir."

"So now that you're on staff, I'll just call you Baker. Is that all right with you, Baker?"

"Sure," I sighed. At least it wasn't *Miss*.

"So, Baker," the Colonel said with a gloating countenance, "you will be our new maid—provisionally. What does that pay, Haynes?"

Haynes murmured, "We budgeted sixty thousand."

The Colonel looked at me. "Does that work for you? Sixty thousand salary?"

Salary? Suddenly this was turning into a permanent thing! I swallowed. I had not foreseen that my appeal might be accepted. But this was a job. A shit job leading to another shit job, but still—a job. I think I smiled.

Then I ran some math. Sixty thousand a year was thirty bucks an hour. In New York City, that barely kept you in ramen noo-dles. *On the other hand, that could cover my rent and student loans, and I'd still have money left over.* I ran the numbers again because I couldn't believe it. *I'll finally be able to focus on writing and get-ting published, and then I'll definitely be prime faculty material.*

A wash of cool relief gave me a shiver down my back.

But then a cascade of realpolitik spilled into my mind: *What about that eviction notice? What good will a job be if you're home-less? If all your stuff is seized and sold off in a flea market?* My heart pounded. *Not much good at all.*

"I—" I cut myself off. I couldn't ask what I was about to ask, could I? I couldn't risk blowing the whole thing. But the Colonel's friendly eyes dashed my qualms. "I just have one more request."

"What's that?" the Colonel asked.

I took a deep breath and thought, *Here goes* . . . "I need an advance."

The silence of the room poured down upon me. Haynes rolled his eyes. But I was committed now, so I pushed on.

"I have rent due and I need to cover it right away."

The Colonel didn't blink. He simply asked, "How much?"

I hesitated. Took a breath. "Ten thousand."

"That's rent these days?"

"Well, four months of it," I said, trying not to grimace.

The Colonel narrowed his eyes. Then nodded. "Done."

Knowing my bank's policies about out-of-town checks, I added, "In certified funds."

The Colonel closed his eyes. "No, we can't do that."

I knew it. I'd pushed it too far. Now I was going to lose out on this opportunity and have to go back home without a job and get evicted.

"There's just no time to get to our bank." He looked to Haynes. "We have that much in petty cash, don't we, Haynes?"

Haynes gave a reluctant nod.

The Colonel faced me. "Would cash be acceptable?"

I was stunned. "Sure." Cash would be perfect!

The Colonel stood up. "Excellent! We're short on time, so Haynes will take you now to do the paperwork and all the details. After everything's over tonight, find me in my office—it's on this level, in the north wing—and I'll give you the advance."

I stood.

He extended his hand.

I took it.

His grasp was dry and warm. He said, "Well! This worked out quite marvelously! Thank you, Baker."

7

Ms. D'Aleu, the Colonel's young and beautiful attorney, had her own sumptuous mahogany-paneled office on the second floor of the same mansion. Her very white skin almost glowed. A tight, thick braid of blue-black hair draped the shoulder of her fine black wool Akris pantsuit. I didn't think I was making a very good first impression as I was having something of a mild panic attack about signing an employment contract she, as the Colonel's attorney, had drawn up.

Right there at the top of the page were the words:

Employee Position: Maid

and I quailed right there.

Silly me. I'd thought I was making a genius move in taking—no, *demanding*—this job. But now, at the moment I had to actually commit to this gambit, an argument broke out in my head. My ego was protesting: *What hubris! I'm not a maid, I'm a scholar! I don't have the skills for this!* But my superego was shouting back: *You must do this! You must take responsibility and get your finances in order, whatever it takes!*

Meanwhile, through it all, my id was screaming: *Run away! Escape while you still can! Before you make a total fool of yourself! Before you lose your soul!*

(It didn't feel so melodramatic at the time. Do people usually have panic attacks when someone gives them exactly what they ask for?)

"Miss Baker—"

"Dr. Baker," I said.

"Is there a problem?" she asked. Her eyes were kind, brown pools of compassion.

I sucked in a deep breath and looked away. On the wall behind her hung a framed Juris Doctor diploma from Columbia, my alma mater. My own PhD looked much the same. But it wasn't the same, was it? Here she had this luxurious office while I was facing eviction from my closet-sized apartment. Her degree made her a lawyer. All my degree could get me was this job as a maid. What would my father say!

I couldn't tell him, of course. He had always pushed me toward law school. *An academic career these days is a pipe dream, Mel,* he would say. *Law is a secure career. People are always doing dishonest things, immoral things, stupid things. People always need lawyers.* To which I would always reply, *Just what I want to do in life—work with cheaters, monsters, and idiots.* To which he would reply, *That's job security.* Which never struck me as a winning argument. Yeah, I was wise.

Staring at Ms. d'Aleu's diploma, I silently I repeated the mantra, *My name is Melody Tess Baker, scholar. I have a PhD and a brain. I am intelligent and capable, a woman worthy of respect. Besides, this is only temporary.*

"Melody—may I call you Melody?" Ms. d'Aleu asked in her silky voice. "If you have any questions about any of the language, I would be happy to go over it with you."

I focused on her. She watched me with a restrained intensity that seemed to pierce right into me. She didn't even smile, but right then she seemed like the nicest lawyer I'd ever met.

Okay, what the fuck. I signed the papers.

She promptly tucked the contract into a drawer. There was no going back now.

Without a word, she walked over to a closet and drew out a black garment bag and shoebox. She handed them to me with a mysterious grin.

8

HAYNES LED ME UP two steep, tortuous flights of winding and worn servants' stairs to a somewhat dingy level with narrow hallways, threadbare carpet, and soiled plaster, and left me in an unused bedroom where I was to change into my uniform. Like the foyer, the bedroom, too, was bigger than my apartment. Three mismatched, bare incandescent bulbs in the ceiling provided the only illumination. A dusty set of gilded and rather garish comedy-tragedy masks decorated the wall, no doubt orphaned by the previous resident who had tired of their company.

Only then did I open the garment bag and see just what I was supposed to wear.

On a padded hangar hung a very short, shiny black dress with crisp white trim that ran along the deep v–shaped collar, as well as around the short sleeves and along the hem. *That's the uniform?* It was nothing at all like the stodgy, lace-trimmed potato sacks you see in *Downton Abbey*. This skimpy thing struck me as more like a Halloween-costume version—except for the fine fabric and double-stitched tailoring.

On the wall, the masks watched me, laughing and crying at the same time as I indulged in a healthy moment of despair. I asked myself, *Am I really going to wear this?* To which I countered, *Can it really be that bad?* This was a paying job. I would have worn the back half of a horse costume for that money.

I glared defiantly back at the masks. *Yes, this is just theater*, I told myself. *Just like dating. I can do this.*

After slipping out of my navy-blue suit, I held the uniform in front of my body. It came to just about mid-thigh. Maybe I could wear this and still maintain some dignity. Unfortunately, the hemline exposed several inches of my midi half-slip. It had to go.

I unbuttoned the back—yes, I said *buttons*—and stepped into the uniform. It slid up snugly over my hips and waist. I poked my hands through the armholes, and the little number was on. The v-neck dipped daringly low, exposing as much cleavage as my swimsuit bikini top does. I was suddenly thankful I had worn a demi-cup cami bra.

Reaching behind in the series of contortion moves from women's clothing yoga, I fastened all seventeen buttons, from the small of my back to the nape of my neck.

The dress fit surprisingly well. Maybe a bit loose in the waist, but Ms. d'Aleu had sized me up pretty well. I wanted to see, but the room in this spare-no-expenses mansion had no mirror, not even on the closet door. *Crap.*

The garment bag's internal zip pouch bulged with something cushy. *Ah*, I figured, *the pantyhose. Probably something modest-*

ly opaque. Inside the pouch were *two* black-plastic-wrapped packages.

I ripped one open: *a garter belt*! I'm not sure, but I think I swore out loud at that point.

(Chad, my ex-boyfriend, had given me one of these for Valentine's Day, except his gift was embellished with powder-pink lace and little custard-colored flowers. Obviously he didn't know me at all. We broke up a week later.)

I held the device up between two fingers. This item was plain black with no lace or brocade—purely functional, not at all one of those frilly garter belts you'd find in The Kiki de Montparnasse—but it still struck me as something out of the nineteenth century.

I hitched the belt around my waist, under the dress, and tore into the other plastic package, where I found the silkiest, shiniest stockings. They felt supple in my hands and wanted to slip like water through my fingers. I held them out and let them drape, and saw that they were very sheer, with seams all the way up.

Seams!

And no elastic thigh band, which explained the garter belt. I supposed thigh-highs would have been too practical.

Or not sexy enough? Was this going to be some kind of kink party tonight? Were all the men going to wear masks and chant arcane Latin verses over the bodies of naked women? Was that why the money was so good?

Resolving not to let my imagination run away from me, I sat, slid the slinky hose onto my legs, and performed some more yoga to fasten them up with the garter straps.

That left the shoes. I opened the shoebox. Inside, nestled in tissue, were a pair of black Manolo Blahnik stiletto pumps with four-and-a-half-inches heels thin as pencils.

For a long, contemplative instant, I considered wearing my own much-more-sensible Mootsies. It went against my better judgment as my shoes were navy, a color *never* to be worn with a black outfit. My mother didn't raise an idiot. But oh, I was tempted. I slipped the Manolos on. Despite the screaming tendons in my ankles, I was able to stand quite easily. In fact, these CFM pumps were more comfortable than my own low-heeled shoes. Go figure.

As I moved, I felt some tugging on the garter straps, pulling the garter belt down. I checked. No, the garter belt wasn't going anywhere. The straps were just holding the stockings in constant tension so that the silk slid across my skin with each step. This was going to take some getting used to.

So there I was, maid for success.

The masks on the wall stared at me in silent comment, one frowning, mocking my self-pity, the other outright laughing at me like I didn't realize that I was the joke.

9

*J*UDGING BY HER FLUSHED cheeks and pinched lips, Madge Metz (who, it turned out, was the underbutler and head parlor maid in charge of the evening's event—drinks, meals, desserts, coffees, teas, and any and all general comforts) did *not at all* like the notion of breaking in at the last minute an inexperienced, awkward maid.

Not five minutes earlier, I had made my way downstairs via the sweeping main staircase to the foyer, where florists were delivering through the wide-open front doors these gorgeous sprays of blooms; the chill draft that followed them in reminded me that yes, I really was more comfortable in jeans, and no, the dress and stockings did not do much to keep my tush warm.

Now among people, I could feel just how provocative was my uniform. But as it turned out, nobody paid me any mind—except when I got in the way of the flower bearers.

Haynes approached. "Miss Baker," he said in a quiet voice that emanated calm, and briefly bowed his head. For a second I thought he was showing me his widow's peak. He then regarded me with his dark eyes, his bearded mahogany face expressionless. Somehow, though, he put me at ease.

"I have a PhD," I said calmly, and smiled to soften the correction. "I'm *Dr.* Baker."

He regarded me with an inscrutable expression. "I understand. You have worked hard for this title, and that deserves respect."

That was more like it. "Thank you."

"In this household," he said, "we in the service staff operate with a polite courtesy. This facilitates smooth interactions between staff, even in stressful situations, and the comfort and ease of our guests. I am properly addressed as Mr. Haynes. The others, whom you soon shall meet, are addressed similarly. I suggest we do not address you as Dr. Baker but rather as Miss Baker, so as not to intimidate others on the staff or, most importantly, our guests—most of whom do not have advanced degrees."

Intimidate others? I held back a mocking laugh, thinking it would be better to come up with a more tactful response. But before I could think of the right pithy-yet-subtle retort to such preposterous logic, he continued, "I and the rest of the household appreciate your consideration."

"Haynes—" I started, then corrected myself. *Polite courtesy.* "Mr. Haynes," I said, fully intending to reject his request—and then my righteous indignation bled out of me like air out of a Thanksgiving parade animal. I asked for this job. I wasn't here to teach literary theory. "Miss Baker will be fine."

Mr. Haynes leaned close. "Perhaps you'd like to know," he murmured, "I have a PhD in mathematics and another in

Greek." He furrowed his brow for emphasis, which convinced
me that he wasn't just goofing on me. The thought enclouded
me with a moment of despair. Is this what PhDs must resort to
just to eat? "Let's just keep that between you and me," he added
and gave me the slightest of smiles.

I smiled in return. We were fellow scholars veiling our minds,
slumming it for the rich.

He tipped his head. "This way." With a stately gait, he led
me to the dining hall, where he introduced me to Ms. Metz,
who, upon learning of my lack of qualifications, huffed with
a nasal Chicago accent, "I need trained people, Mr. Haynes.
We're going to have twenty-four guests tonight and I'm *at least*
four shy of a proper staff. I don't understand why it's so hard
to find people."

"It's harder to find them than to fire them," Mr. Haynes said,
sotto voce.

"I fire them because they're incompetent!" Ms. Metz hissed.
Her agitation was almost electric. About fifty, slender, and,
judging by her wiry muscle tone and rosy skin color, physically
fit—certainly in better shape than I—Ms. Metz wore her uniform, identical to mine, with a casual indifference. But then I
noticed that her hose were opaque black tights, not sheer stockings, and they had no seams, either. Maybe rank had privilege.
Maybe she had varicose veins.

She dropped her voice. "Did you see how that redhead, the
one with the stripper name—"

Mr. Haynes looked away. "Ms. Bambi."

"—the way Bambi served that plate to the Princess Talagaka—"

Mr. Haynes closed his eyes as if touched by a painful memory.

Ms. Metz continued: "—and spilled peas off the plate and they rolled to the middle of the table? I. Was. Mortified!"

Mr. Haynes put a white-gloved finger between closed eyes.

Ms. Metz craned her neck forward. "All through that dinner, I couldn't stop looking at those peas just lying there, mocking the integrity of this house." She closed her eyes and calmed herself. "The Academy had no qualified candidates?"

"There is much competition."

"Not even new graduates from Colorado or Ohio?"

Mr. Haynes folded his hands behind his back.

Ms. Metz put her hands on her hips. "We've been under-staffed for six months now."

"I understand."

"And so today we have Brick-house Betty here"—that would be me—"when who I really need is another Ms. Odette, another Mrs. Phillips, another Ms. Vitiello, and another me, because one of each of us isn't enough."

"Anyway," Mr. Haynes bowed his head, "the decision is mine."

Most people would have been quite content to let the blame rest with the boss and position themselves as virtuous by comparison. Right then I had a new respect for Mr. Haynes.

"So it's on you when she fudges everything up." She looked at me. "Nothing personal."

I gave her my smile of accommodation.

Ms. Metz asked Mr. Haynes, "What can she do?" Before he could answer, she turned to me. "What can you do?"

My mouth went dry. I swallowed.

But before I could answer, she waved me off. "Never mind.

We'll work it out. We're running out of time. Guests arrive in fifty-three minutes."

Mr. Haynes gave me a look I couldn't read, then gracefully turned and walked out of the dining hall.

Ms. Metz put her hands on her hips and looked me up and down. "Christ, I never knew our uniforms could work so hard."

Up until that point, I didn't think I could have felt any more awkward, but now I wanted to wrap myself up in the tablecloth.

She sighed. "The Colonel and Mr. Haynes saw something in you—god only knows what—but here you are, and we've got work to do."

She grasped one of my hands and examined it intently on all sides. What now? A palm reading? *You will go on a long ocean voyage!* Instead, she tut-tutted and said, "Our nail tech won't come until Tuesday. You'll need to do your own nails."

"I didn't bring any polish with—"

"We'll get you some. I assume you've waited tables."

"Yes."

"Nice place or greasy spoon?"

"Nice places."

"What about cocktail waitress?"

"No."

"Good. What we do is discreet. I don't want any pole-dancer vibe in the dining room."

"Of course not."

"Well, we won't have you serve dinner until we have time to rehearse."

Rehearse?

"It's far too complicated," she said.

Too complicated? How complicated could serving dinner be? But I didn't argue.

"What can you do? Champagne? I don't know. Wine? Maybe. Cocktails? Yes, but the boys usually pour their own. Smokes?"

She led me to the side table and picked up an ornate, jewel-encrusted gold elephant. It was hideously beautiful; I loved it as soon as I saw it.

She smiled conspiratorially. "Isn't he delightful? Here, you squeeze his belly," she said, squeezing, and an orange flame sparked to life from the elephant's trunk. A toothy joy lit up her face; she said with affection, "This is Milo."

"Pleased to meet you, Milo."

"The Colonel brought him back from Bali. He brings us luck."

We both admired Milo for a few seconds.

Then the smile was gone and she was back to business. "If you see a guest preparing to light up—a cigarette, a cigar, a pipe, a doobie—well, probably leave him alone if he's sparking a doobie—you silently and gracefully provide the light."

I nodded. "I'll be a lighting mime."

"Rules," she said and held up a finger. "Never address the guest from behind and surprise him."

"Right, don't talk."

"*Address*, as in *approach*."

Only an hour on the job and my vocabulary was already expanding.

She put up a second finger. "Don't bow down in front of a gentleman and give him a peek at your cleavage."

"Easier said, given these uniforms."

"Approach in his line of sight, but step to his side before pouring or lighting or whatever you're there to do." She raised a third finger. "And don't chat with them. Boundaries, Miss Baker. Boundaries."

"Boundaries."

"The guests will speak to you, but they don't want to hear from you, aside from, 'Yes, sir,' or, 'Yes, ma'am.' They have their own conversations. It's best not to listen."

"My ears are sealed."

"You're quite the comedienne."

"Not really."

"Servants don't joke."

"Never."

"I'm not joking."

"I can tell."

She narrowed her eyes at me and said, "The thing to remember is: It's never about you."

"No."

"Don't express an opinion."

"No."

"Don't interrupt."

"Of course not."

"What do you do if someone compliments the food?"

Quiz time? "Well, I would thank them—"

"No."

"No?"

"Never accept a compliment," she said.

"Never accept a compliment?"

"I know, it sounds impossible, but it's really quite simple: If you accept a compliment, you're making it about you, and that would be inappropriate."

"Thank goodness," I cracked out of nerves. *No*, I was thinking. *Why would I ever want to accept a compliment?*

"Nothing is ever about you," Ms. Metz said.

"Right. Everything is *you*-less." I couldn't help myself.

"When someone compliments you—for example, a guest compliments you on the wine you're pouring—you curtsy and tell them you will pass along their compliment to the Colonel."

"And do I?"

"Do you what?"

"Pass the compliment along to the Colonel."

"No, of course not! Pass it along to *me*—or Mr. Haynes—and if it's appropriate, *we* will inform the Colonel."

"Right."

"Let's say you're bringing a guest a cocktail and he is clumsy reaching for it and knocks it over, spilling over himself. What do you do?"

What do I do? "I would . . . apologize and—"

"No."

"No?"

"Never apologize."

That stumped me. "Because it's a sign of weakness?"

"Because, again, it makes it about *you*. Nobody cares about your feelings. Your remorse, even if sincere, is not relevant."

"So what should I do in that situation?"

She counted off on three fingers. "You *assess*, *inform*, and *act*. Does he need a towel to clean himself up? If so, you inform him that you will fetch a towel and then you do so."

"Why wouldn't I apologize?" I asked, trying to wrap my brain around this. "Isn't that just good manners?"

"Apologies are about ego. Good manners is leaving the guests to their own thoughts. By letting them know that you're taking care of the problem, you give them some relief to their anxiety of the moment, without forcing them to deal with your feelings. That," Ms. Metz said, "is good manners."

I puzzled over that one as I pictured myself on the streets of New York, bumping into somebody and spilling coffee all over them, and then not apologizing so they didn't have to deal with my feelings. *Yeah, that would go over real well.*

"You need to pay attention here." Ms. Metz was scowling.

"Sorry." She gave me a look. *Oh, that's right. Never apologize!* "Sorry." This was going to take some practice.

Ms. Metz took a deep breath. "Look," she said, "this may seem difficult at first, but any conversation you have with the guests is simply to facilitate you serving them. And nothing more. No 'Some weather we're having!' or 'How 'bout them Yankees!'"

I waved a hand in reassurance. "Oh, I never pay attention to baseball, anyway."

"The real conversation, the one you should always be paying attention to, is the one we—you and I and the rest of service—have with each other."

"In the kitchen?"

Ms. Metz visibly hid her exasperation. "No, the conversation we have while we serve. The conversation with our eyes." She counted off on three fingers. "We *watch*, we *anticipate*, we *serve*."

I absorbed that. "We are the gears that keep polite society moving smoothly," I said.

"We're not gears, Miss Baker." She smiled with her eyes. "We're dancers." She counted off on three fingers. "We *plan*, we *choreograph*, we *rehearse*. Like dancers onstage, we work with each other, we move in harmony, each of us performing our role. But unlike dancers onstage, we're not the show. The family and guests are the show; they perform for each other. Do you understand?"

It sounded beautiful. "I'm ready," I said; inspired, I actually felt it.

"Take off those earrings," Ms. Metz said.

I gave her my good-luck earrings—the dangling silver pilcrows. She handed me small pearl studs to shove into my earlobes.

"Let me see you curtsy."

I gave her my never-was-a-debutante best.

The look on her face shattered my bravado.

10

FIVE MINUTES LATER, the castle was bustling. Guests arrived in rapid succession, at first sashaying like stars on the red carpet at the Oscars, except older, stuffier, and more conservative—and probably richer. But then with the darkening evening, heavy snow started to fall, lending the procession a degree of urgency, with people scurrying up the dozen or so marble steps from the doors of their limos to the doors of the mansion.

As if heralding the arrival of royalty, Mr. Haynes formally announced each guest by honorific and name as they entered. Several of them greeted him back.

I tried to memorize their names while Mrs. Phillips—a white-haired woman with pink skin, a million freckles and forty-five years in service—and I collected their damp overcoats, furs, hats, and a few umbrellas, all of which we stowed on long racks in a walk-in coat-check closet that was also bigger than my entire apartment.

"The gentleman's and the lady's together," said Mrs. Phillips while I was trying to one-arm wrestle a twenty-pound chinchilla onto a large wooden hanger. "We try to keep them alphabetical, but it's best to just remember where you put each one."

The chinchilla finally surrendered, and I had two hands to deal with a heavy wool coat and fluffy gray fox fur stole.

At one point, a commotion erupted in the foyer. Two gentlemen shouted at each other in that way old acquaintances do when remoteness is replaced with proximity and excitement.

"Hal!" cried one Mr. Renaldo Mercuria, a husky middle-aged gentleman with black mutton chops that used up all the hair that should have been on top of his head.

Mr. Henry Yves, a sallow, gaunt gentleman with a wild mane of silver curls, growled back, "Rennie!"

They slapped each other on the shoulders and laughed at their good fortune. "I heard you're now at that think tank. What are you doing there?" asked Mr. Yves.

"I think they want me to think!" cracked Mr. Mercuria, and they both roared.

"Excuse me," said a youngish, attractive-yet-severe-looking woman in a Brooks Brothers business suit as she pushed right between them. The gentlemen watched, dumbstruck, as the olive-complected brunette handed me her mink-collared overcoat, lambskin gloves, and a Maison Michel fedora. With a glance at the gentlemen, she said, "Boys," and strode away.

Mr. Yves bent close to Mr. Mercuria. "Was that—?"

"Yes," said Mr. Mercuria with a sage nod. "They must be serious."

"He's really running, isn't he?"

Mr. Mercuria coughed. "This, my friend, is going to require strong spirits."

And the two gentlemen ambled off in search of liquor, leaving me wondering, *Who's running? Running for what?*

"Let me see the hat," Mrs. Phillips said. I handed it to her, and with what looked like a sponge brush she carefully wicked the moisture off of the top. "When you wipe a hat, you must take care with it. Some hats are very soft and can lose their structure. If you leave them wet, they can warp or even stain." She finished and handed the hat back to me; I placed it on top of the rack, above the overcoat. "When we're busy, you can hang the coats first and brush them out after, but it's best not to wait with a hat."

A few seconds later, the Honorable Matilda MacDougal-Oglethorpe—a well-regarded judge, I later learned—flounced in cradling a cute little orange Pomeranian to match her mink and her hair. She held the fuzzball out to me. "Here, take her a moment," she said, so I reached out—and the little yapper growled and snapped at me. "Hey, there, baby-wayby," she cooed at the pup. "Don't bite the maid or I'll have to buy the Colonel another."

I was about to say something injudicious to the Honorable Matilda MacDougal-Oglethorpe—something that probably would've gotten me jailed for contempt—when Mr. Haynes stepped into the role of hero and carefully took charge of the feral menace to carry it away.

"No snacks!" the Honorable Matilda MacDougal-Oglethorpe barked at his back. "If she touches anything non-organic, she won't poop for days!"

By the time we were finished checking all the coats, hats, scarves, stoles, capes, earmuffs, umbrellas, and gloves, the cocktails and champagne were in full swing for the twenty or so guests.

Ms. Metz pressed an opened bottle of Dom into my hands. "This is against my better judgment, but everyone else is busy. Walk through the rooms. Refill anyone who's down to a third of a glass." Her voice dropped to a whisper. "But fill only to two-thirds."

I nodded and she was gone to handle other things, so I walked into the great library, where a fire roared and popped in the five-foot-high hearth, offering some warmth in the cold company. Only two hours before, I'd entered this great room in desperate pursuit of a survival job; now I was on the hunt for under-filled crystal flutes.

One of the hardest things about being big, not just tall, is that high heels present a problem. I'm five-eleven in bare feet. Put me into four-and-a-half-inch heels, I'm looking down at ninety-five percent of men and pretty much all women—even if *they're* in heels. And I'm in constant fear of spearing someone's foot. But when it comes down to it, I really just don't like drawing attention to myself in a vampy outfit. I'm more of a nerd. Give me flats and of course my black leather jacket (New York armor) and I'm happy.

So here I was in a short dress, towering over everyone; and yet to these people of importance, I was practically invisible. Not simply unnoticed—*beneath* notice. To be honest, it was something of a relief.

If only it worked this way on the streets of Manhattan.

Laughter erupted on the far side of the room as a gentleman waved his arms, relating to three other gentlemen what must have been a truly amusing anecdote.

I spotted an under-filled-flute target not ten feet away. The gentleman holding the champagne flute glanced over and I smiled, holding up the bottle to indicate my intentions. He swung his glass ever so slightly toward me and continued talking. "We still have twelve days to file our petitions with the Board of Elections. So all we need, aside from money, are signatures."

"Oh, that's all," someone said dryly.

"This isn't an insurmountable problem," the empty-glass gentleman said and launched into a detailed treatise on the various processes one might employ to collect thousands of voter signatures in a hurry.

As he spoke, his glass wavered. I tried to track the movement with the bottle—but I may have been a bit distracted, pondering how what he was saying connected with the election talk I'd heard in the foyer, so when his hand paused, I poured—and totally misjudged how full the bottle was.

Champagne sloshed like Yosemite Falls into the flute, triggering a bubbling eruption of fizzing Dom Pérignon that gushed out all over his hand.

Unthinkingly I offered a quiet apology.

He scowled at me, turned his back, switched the glass to his other hand, and shook the champagne off of his fingers, and said to the others, "We're quite fortunate that Detton died when he did."

This was when Detton's name first came up that evening—at least that I heard.

"If he had died next week, for instance, we would have been fucked."

Mortified—not about Detton's death but my apology *faux pas*—I retreated, leaving them alone to sort out the political advantages of unexpected death.

Ms. Vitiello met me in the corner.

"Never talk to the clients," she whispered.

"It was an accident," I said.

She flashed me a look of *Are you fucking kidding me?* "The Colonel doesn't approve of accidents." And with that, she drifted away.

Right, nobody approves of accidents . . . unless there's political advantage in it.

11

THE HUBBUB OF VOICES was replaced by susurration. All eyes turned toward the doorway, where Mr. Haynes announced to everyone, "Mr. Theodore Miller Snoot."

Next to him, a thirty-something white man, clean in a fresh-scrubbed way, trim in his charcoal Italian suit, well-groomed, with a muff of straight chestnut hair on top of his head, muttered out the side of his mouth, ventriloquist-like: "Teddy."

Mr. Haynes said, "Mr. Theodore *'Teddy'* Miller Snoot."

Theodore "Teddy" Miller Snoot grinned and strutted into the room as if he was the guest of honor arriving fashionably late. *This must be the guy running for office.* I immediately took a dislike to him. I'd seen his kind before—colleagues of my father—you know, those guys who carry themselves everywhere on a cloud of smugness from believing they could buy anything they saw; and it was his eyes that claimed possession over me as soon as they found me.

Uh oh, I thought, *trouble coming.*

He crossed directly over to me. We stood eye to eye. His jutting chin and perfect teeth were a perfect complement to his melodious baritone. "So you're the new girl. What happened to Bambi?"

I think I had a pretty good idea now. "I don't know," I said. "I can go find out."

He cut off my escape and leaned close. "You're the most beautiful thing in this musty old castle." He smelled like burnt popcorn. I couldn't breathe.

"Teddy," someone said, "leave the help alone."

Teddy ignored him and gave me a predatory smile. He said in a quiet voice of intimacy, "Get me a Bloody Mary, would you, babe?"

The Colonel may have been backing him, but Teddy Snoot wasn't going to get my vote. I performed my smiling curtsy and escaped toward the bar, trying to calm my racing heart. A few steps away, Mr. Forbin and Mr. Threwsbury, of a generation that tends to find amusement in these sorts of transgressions, gave me winks of approval.

From what I could see, the Colonel wasn't much of a vodka man and had no premade mix. I made my way into the kitchen for some tomato juice and celery stalks, which I found inside the walk-in cooler.

A hand cradled my ass.

I whirled, but a strong arm pulled me up into his chest.

Teddy Snoot had no smile now. "The only way to get rid of a temptation is to yield to it," he said.

I raised an eyebrow. "Oscar Wilde? Really?"

"No, I'm Teddy," he said, apparently serious.

"You know, things didn't work out so well for Dorian Gray."

"Good you got rid of him." He tugged me close. "I want to know who you are."

What a perfect politician: all teeth and no brains. I held my poise. "I'm Miss Baker." I wasn't going to give him the satisfaction of knowing I was a fallen PhD.

"What's your first name?"

"You can just call me Miss Baker."

"You can call me Teddy if you give me a kiss." His eyes burned into me and I felt my face flush. His skin gleamed under the fluorescent lights. He'd missed a spot shaving just under his bottom lip. I wanted to bite that dumb pink flesh.

He planted his face on mine with a hard kiss. An active tongue thrust past my teeth.

I pushed against his chest but he held me tight. I bit down, but his tongue slipped away. He grinned, which only enraged me more. Then he glommed on to my breast.

I grabbed his hand and wrenched against his thumb, but that was only partially successful. "Mr. Snoot. Let. Go."

"You can call me Teddy now. You earned it."

He released me, said, "Bring me my drink," patted my ass, and strutted out.

I was shaking. My lower lip was raw where his bristle had rubbed. All of a sudden it felt hot in that walk-in cooler.

So he wants me to bring him a drink? I'll bring him a drink!

I mixed a Bloody Mary Plus—the plus being extra doses of cayenne and horseradish—and made my way back out to the library.

Teddy Snoot had already inserted himself into conversation

with the Colonel and Mr. Henderson—probably looking for a big campaign donation and sucking up to the men with big checkbooks. As I approached, he completely ignored me. *How coy.* I set coaster and glass on the table next to him and crossed the room to check on the other guests.

Mr. Yves waved me over. "Do you know the drink 'black rose?'" I puzzled over that, thinking he'd said *black crows*, which sounded revolting. He whispered, "Bourbon with a dash of Peychaud's and grenadine." That sounded scrumptious. I could have used one of those just then.

I smiled and curtsied and went to the bar to mix the cocktail.

And I glanced over at Teddy Snoot. Cheeks flushed, he flashed a wink at me and slurped his now half-empty cocktail. The arrogant shit.

Obviously I hadn't put in *nearly* enough horseradish.

12

*M*ISS! *OH, WHAT'S YOUR* name? Miss maid!"

The voice, somewhere between a screech and a cackle, cut through the chatter, capturing my attention twenty feet away. It came from Mrs. Pegglesworth, who'd arrived wearing a lime-green plastic poncho to protect her intricately stitched silk kimono, which she'd gone on about acquiring on a monthlong stay in Japan, and which made her the center of exuberant attention from the other guests for the first ten minutes after her colorful entrance. "Konichiwa!" she had cried out several times, bowing in a hunched manner as if she was looking for something she'd dropped on the floor.

Mrs. Pegglesworth herself had been Honorable, but apparently no longer. Upon their arrival earlier, her husband, the Honorable Roman Sinjin Pegglesworth, FSO, Former Ambassador of the United States to a country in Africa that no longer exists, had snapped at Mr. Haynes for addressing Mrs. Pegglesworth as *Mrs.*

"My lovely wife, to whom I've had the pleasure of being married fifty-two years," the Honorable Roman Sinjin Pegglesworth had declared with a sniff, "was granted a life peerage by Her Majesty, and shall be addressed as *Lady* Pegglesworth or *the Right Honorable Margaret Baroness* Pegglesworth!"

—To which the Right Honorable Margaret Baroness Pegglesworth had waggled her hand and made some kind of coughing noise indicating dismissal of all that. "I'm an American citizen now, my dear. I wish you'd let it go."

The Honorable Roman Sinjin Pegglesworth had then said in a low voice, "But it's your right, my dear. It's a matter of respect."

At that, she had laughed. "I'm quite content to be a Mrs.—in fact, I insist upon it, Pickles." She gave her husband a deep kiss.

And that had been that.

So when I reached the table of Mrs. Pegglesworth, where she was now playing some kind of card game that might have been Baccarat or Crazy Eights with three women—who themselves were dressed not in kimono but merely satin gowns and pearls—I said simply, with my unpracticed curtsy, "Yes, ma'am?"

Mrs. Pegglesworth placed a knuckly hand on my arm, and with that look of desperation in her eyes people get when they are not quite as drunk as they wish to be, she said, "Miss maid, we've had enough of this champagne. We need martinis. You *can* make martinis, can't you?"

Okay, so the black rose threw me, but what self-respecting survivor of grad school would not know how to make a mean martini? "Yes, I can, ma'am," I said. "Gin?"

"Yes! Plymouth's, if the Colonel has it. Some proper British gin!"

The woman to her left whispered fervently, "Plymouth's was bought out. They're owned by *the French* now."

Not wanting to hear it, Mrs. Pegglesworth snapped, "Oh, shut up, Dellie."

I asked, "Olive or a twist?"

"Did I *ask* for a fruit punch?" Her eyes bulged with indignation. This wasn't the time to point out that olive is a fruit, too.

"Same for everyone here?"

They all nodded, even Dellie the Francophobe.

Still clutching my wrist, Mrs. Pegglesworth said, "We need those drinks pronto!" And then she released me and waved her kimonoed arm in dismissal.

She and her friends watched me in silence when I arrived with the large shaker and poured a round into two-ounce crystal cocktail glasses. As I started to pull away, Mrs. Pegglesworth grabbed my arm again. "You're new."

"Yes, ma'am."

"Girl! Girl!" a redheaded man called out from across the room.

Mrs. Pegglesworth held on, locking eyes with me. "If you're going to be serving us, we need to know what to call you."

"Miss Baker, ma'am."

She looked me up and down. "You're a looker, Baker. I bet you have to beat them off with a cricket bat!"

Did that count as a compliment? Was I to pass that along? I decided probably not.

Mrs. Pegglesworth laughed. "When I was your age, I was a looker, too. Not as curvy above the corset, though."

Corset? I'm glad nobody does that anymore—except maybe for kink.

"Girl! Over here!" the man shouted, waving his arm.

I figured he meant me. I started to turn away, but Mrs. Pegglesworth tightened her grip, crushing my wrist with the strength of a woman who secretly goes bowling, and said, "Now hold on while I taste this martini." She let go of my wrist and, with a theatrical flourish, lifted her glass to her lips. "Mmm!" She looked at me. "You know what you're doing, Baker. Keep these coming!"

I smiled and curtsied.

"Girl! Girl!" said the redheaded man as he approached, obviously not wishing to wait another moment. "I'm sorry, I don't know your name."

I hadn't seen him arrive, so I didn't know his name, either. "Miss Baker," I said, and then gave into impulse. "But I'll answer to *Girl! Girl!* if you forget."

He pressed his lips together . . . and a lovely dribble of brown tobacco juice leaked out; he casually swept it away with a stained, monogrammed hankie. "We in the back are in some need of more of that forty-year-old Islay Scotch." A clump of chaw tumbled out as he spoke.

I pretended not to notice and curtsied, then turned to find Mr. Haynes right in front of me, holding a bottle filled with caramel-colored liquid.

"For you," he said.

I thanked him without thinking (thus burdening him with my emotions) and carried the whisky to the circle of men seated with the woman in the Brooks Brothers suit toward the back of the library. The redheaded leaf masticator, of course, did not acknowledge me as I filled his crystal snifter.

"Our challenge," the Brooks Brothers woman said, "is that we don't have much time."

"Five weeks," said another. I kept my eyes on the topping-up task.

"No time for any proper fund-raising."

"The Party has funds."

This sounded interesting, somewhat like the conversations my father had with his backers and strategists—except these gentlemen wore nicer suits and drank much better liquor. I looked for other glasses in need of forty-year-old Scotch so I could listen in.

"Oh, this is good stuff," said Mr. Henderson. "Pour me some more of that, honey."

Sure thing, snookums. I filled his glass with a polite smile on my face.

"Do we have any PACs in place, Ms. Thorndike?" someone asked.

"That will sort itself out," said the Brooks Brothers woman— apparently Ms. Thorndike, who seemed the most savvy of any of them. She was clearly a wonk. *They should be running her instead of Teddy.* "Meanwhile," she added, "we will get private donations and Party funding."

Glasses filled, I took a step back and lingered, ostensibly on standby for refills.

"What strings come," said Mr. Henderson with a hiccup, "with that Party money?"

"Miss, I'd like more of that Scotch," said Ms. Thorndike. I filled her glass. She flashed me an almost-sincere smile and then totally ignored me, instead focusing her sharp eyes on

Mr. Henderson as she said, "Well, the Party, of course, has its platform."

"Exactly!" said Mr. Henderson. He flopped heavily back into his chair. "Platform strings."

"There are always strings," said a familiar voice. Mr. Teddy Snoot sat curled up like a sad dog in a leather armchair tucked up against the drapes.

I resisted the impulse to dump the rest of this no doubt very expensive Scotch onto his head. If he came close to me, he would get his due. Meanwhile, out of perverse curiosity, I listened closely to learn everything I could about the jerk's campaign.

"I don't care about strings," Mr. Mercuria said, "as long as we secure free trade. They act like the people don't want free trade. Who doesn't want free trade? Free trade creates wealth and wealth creates jobs. Everybody benefits!"

The others murmured agreement with this pithy bit of genius economic insight and gulped their drinks.

I stepped in to refill.

"Free trade is part of the platform," said Ms. Thorndike with a note of reassurance.

"And cutting taxes?" asked Pickles.

"Of course."

"We have another challenge," Sir Edward Snickerton Wallis, a narrow, stiff gentleman with a narrow, stiff mustache, said in a stuffy English accent. "The scandal."

"Old Pip's dead, the dumb bastard," said someone else.

"Pip Detton is very much alive in the news," said Sir Edward. "Dominatrices. Drugs. Government contracts."

That created a bit of a stir among these men of breeding. Everyone started talking.

"Government contracts? I hadn't heard that."

"It was in the *Post*."

"Which *Post*? New York? Washington?"

"The Cedar Springs *Post*—what do you think which *Post*?"

"Detton was a parasite."

"Detton was an orniphile!"

"The *Observer* said the rumors that he was involved in parrot smuggling were unsubstantiated."

"Which *Observer*? Charlotte?"

"That's not what I read in the *Times*."

"Which *Times*?"

"What does it matter which *Times*? I read what I read."

Sir Edward raised his voice to resume his proclamation. "We have an image problem, gentlemen. The Party faithful may not turn out for *anyone* we field."

"The Party faithful," Mr. Henderson muttered, and threw back the last of his whisky.

I refilled him.

"Well, whatever the case," said Teddy, "we'll obviously trounce Milford and win the seat." So confident.

Sir Edward removed his nose from his glass. "Milford is a formidable opponent."

"And he's playing to the populist wave," Ms. Thorndike added, "attacking our base for its success."

Mr. Yves said, "It's more communism."

"Socialism," whispered Mr. Mercuria.

Mr. Yves flipped his hand. "Details!"

"You guys are all worked up for nothing," said Mr. Henderson between sips. "Melvin Milford is a nonentity."

"I might remind you that he's a nonentity whose campaign has forty million in the exchequer," said Sir Edward.

"Banks, Ed," Mr. Henderson said. "We call them banks."

Across the room, Ms. Metz was watching me. She gave me a follow-me look—a conversation of eyes—and walked away. I left the bottle.

13

IN THE KITCHEN, Mr. Haynes and the five maids—I, Ms. Metz, Mrs. Phillips, Ms. Vitiello, and Ms. Odette, a teacher who had immigrated from Jamaica but couldn't make ends meet on a public school salary—watched intently as Mrs. Skovde provided a Swedish-accented description of the components as she carefully served out each portion of the first course—"Seared ahi medallions with rucola and goat cheese," topped with "a delicately whipped orange-peanut vinaigrette"— onto the ornate china plates lined up along the twenty-foot worktable. "They would best love this!" Her inflamed rosacea suggested some uncertainty on the matter.

Nobody responded, and I got the definite sense that response was not only unnecessary but perhaps even unwelcome.

She topped each dish with a small amount of brilliant red tobiko. "Now careful on this one," she said with a bit of a lilt. "The roe may slip off the top if you tilt too much."

"We'll be careful, as always, Chef," said Ms. Metz.

"I know you will." Mrs. Skovde wiped her hands on her apron. "Well, be off with you," she said, waving a hand as if sending children out to play.

I stood by as each server used white napkins to pick up a plate in each hand.

Ms. Metz said to me, "You watch closely tonight how it's done. You'll get to do it next time."

Imagine how I strained to withhold my excitement.

She smiled almost dreamily. "It's movement. It's grace! When we're fully staffed and have time to rehearse, it's magic!"

"And the guests, they never notice," said Ms. Odette with a touch of a Jamaican accent.

Ms. Metz laughed. "That's the beauty of it. It's The Dance everybody sees, but only we can appreciate." She grinned with eyes sparkling.

I came in on the refrain. "The family and guests are performing for each other."

Mr. Haynes raised an eyebrow at me. Ms. Metz nodded, and they moved toward the dining room door.

"One point for the new girl," whispered Ms. Vitiello. She gave me a conspiratorial wink. I groaned inside but did my best to project excitement with my face.

As the staff commenced the serving of the ahi salads, I noticed that not only Ms. Metz but all the other maids wore black opaque hose. I was the only one in sheer stockings! *Was there a mix-up with my uniform?*

As they performed The Dance—a waltz both languid and precise, in sync, with a grace that melted some of my well-honed, city-cultivated jadedness—I followed along with the

steps in my head: *One plate in each hand, stand behind the lady;
on cue, and in unison, serve the plate to the lady from the left; then
glissade to the right while shifting the other plate to the left; then
serve the gentleman.*

The coordinated presentation was actually a joy to behold,
but the diners saw only the food placed under their noses. And
one another.

With not half of the table served, conversation continued
as courtesy dictated while the staff returned to the kitchen
for the next run; and with the second sortie from kitchen to
table, which left only the two pair of guests seated at the table
ends without plates, the confabulation diminished in anticipation of the banquet. I was reminded of when I was growing
up, how Gertrude and George, our rambunctious Rhodesian
Ridgebacks, would always wait quietly and patiently, pretend-
ing to be well behaved while their dog dishes were being filled.
Anticipation of food quiets the minds of all species.

Once Ms. Vitiello and Mrs. Phillips brought out the last four
plates, the murmur dissolved into occasional individual remarks
as forks clinked on china.

Teddy Snoot took a bite and said with his mouth full, "Now
that's what I call a salad!" It didn't quite register with me at the
time the significance of Mr. Snoot's seat at the last-served end
of the table, far from the Colonel in the middle.

We all—except for Mr. Haynes, who remained to watch for
unexpected needs—retired to the kitchen.

"That was okay," said Ms. Metz. "Ms. Vitiello, you're still
ritardando on the hand shift. *Tempo allegretto.*"

Ms. Vitiello pressed her lips together.

"What did you see, Miss Baker?" asked Ms. Metz.

"I liked how you held the second plate stationary as you shifted hands and stepped to the next person."

Ms. Metz beamed. "Mr. Haynes brought us that. He learned it in the Marines."

That explained his poise, his gait, his reserve. *Is the Colonel from the Marine Corps, too? Is that where they met?*

As if summoned, Mr. Haynes stepped in through the door. "More claret," he said, drawing a key from his pocket as he stepped to a door at the far end. He turned the dead bolt and descended a dark staircase.

While Ms. Odette and Ms. Vitiello cleared empty salad plates, Ms. Metz drew me aside. "Next course, watch the footwork. Learn the steps."

"I will," I said. This was actually exciting, like doing the hokeypokey.

She handed me a heavy crystal pitcher. "And keep everyone's water filled."

As we all slipped back into the dining room, Pickles was elocuting on the noble calling of public service: "The politician subsumes his interest below the interests of his constituents. That is why some love him and so many hate him. Those that love him do so because of his dedication and vision, while those who hate him do so because they can only be disappointed. Rare is the politician who delights everyone." Pickles sipped his wine. "Mmmm-mmmm!" he hummed and swallowed. "And if you come across a politician who delights everyone," he added with extra force in his voice, "make sure you live outside his jurisdiction!"

The guests all laughed pleasantly. The service staff stoically commenced service of the soup, and I saw that Ms. Metz was right: The steps of The Dance were where the magic lay. *Present; left forward, left back; right to the right, left together; right to the right, left together; left forward, left back; exeunt.*

Mr. Haynes went through the moves with crisp, yet somehow easy precision.

On the other hand, Ms. Metz performed with a dancer's grace, each step more of a pause than a full stop.

Ms. Vitiello was so light-footed in her motions, she almost didn't seem to touch the floor.

Ms. Odette's feet were like water: fluid in motion, effortless in settling.

Mrs. Phillips's footwork appeared to be second nature; I later learned that she had been doing the military presentation service style since she worked in the governor's mansion back in the last century.

If I was to learn this and be able to do it with unobtrusive style, I was going to need practice. I mentally ran through the steps while topping up water glasses. And listening.

Teddy said, "My Ferrari was delivered today!"

"Oh," said Sir Edward, "so you like what the Italians make, do you?"

"I got the new Berlinetta. Has a V12, purrs like nothing else."

Mr. Henderson said, "If you like that kind of thing."

"Why wouldn't you?"

"I like something I can get around in."

Teddy Snoot practically sneered. "You mean like a Jeep?"

"I mean a cat that can get you through anything. But if you

need something street-legal," Mr. Henderson said, "the Bentley Bentayga is the car you want. Ferraris are for peasants."

Teddy Snoot's face reddened. "Ferrari makes the finest cars anywhere!"

"Show me how fine your Ferrari does in a snowstorm, Mario," Mr. Henderson said and threw back a mouthful of wine.

I stifled my own snicker. Teddy Snoot may have been their candidate, but they sure didn't seem to like him.

As the serving of the main course began, I couldn't help but notice that Ms. Thorndike, seated next to the Colonel, was espousing to him something in hushed tones and at some length. I did my best to open my ears wide, but Mrs. Pegglesworth and Mrs. Beaulieu were conversing voluminously over the finer points of queen's-gambit chess openings, and several others were in their own tête-à-têtes. Of Ms. Thorndike's disquisition, I could hear only emphatic mumbling. She was obviously saying something of import. What was her role in this affair? From what I could tell, she wasn't the spouse of any other guest.

"Miss Baker," said Ms. Metz in a hushed voice. "The cheese platter wants some attention."

14

*I*T TURNED OUT THAT the cheese platter in the other room didn't need just attention, it needed life support. I swept the crumbs and cheese blobs off the tablecloth into a napkin and fetched from the kitchen a platter of particularly crusty cheese freshly laid out by Mrs. Skovde.

From there I was in constant motion, pouring strong after-dinner cocktails, serving small plates of a particularly pungent chèvre, assisting a wobbly Mrs. Trimbleberry to the washroom, fetching a lap blanket for the Honorable Zachary Trimbleberry, and busing dirty plates.

Yet my mind remained fixed upon those political gentlemen, who had circled up again. Judging by their faces, I just knew they were discussing something significant and world-altering. I strove to find a way to insinuate myself into earshot, but the demands of the guests kept me in the dark.

A short while later, while I was replacing the cheese with chocolate truffle strawberries, the huddle broke, and the various gentlemen wandered off into other conversations, all so very casual. Something was up, but I couldn't discern what.

Mr. Haynes walked by, pausing only briefly to say, "Ice."

In the kitchen, I shoveled large-cubed ice from the machine into a utilitarian metal canister and rushed out to the cocktail table, where I had to stop in my tracks. Standing in my way and quite effectively, if incidentally, blocking access to the large and empty silver ice tureen, the Honorable Matilda MacDougal-Oglethorpe was very slowly and deliberately measuring out portions of various liquors into two cocktail glasses. I had to wait.

"I learned this from a farm girl at Radcliffe," she said to Mr. Rosington, a lanky, whiskery gentleman imported from Texas and, judging by his complexion, soused for several decades.

"Indeed," he said politely.

"Say what you want," the Honorable Matilda MacDougal-Oglethorpe said, "but peasants can come up with marvelous food and drink! Now for the rum." She scrutinized the bottles before her.

The ice canister in my hands was dripping with condensation. To avoid getting wetter than I already was, I held it away from my body.

Mr. Rosington turned to me. "Are you the lovely new addition to the Colonel's staff?"

"First night," I said.

"Here, allow me," he said and took the canister from my hands—and immediately lost his grip.

It fell with a crash. Ice skittered across the rug and clattered on the hardwood floor.

"Well, that will not do!" said the Honorable Matilda
MacDougal-Oglethorpe.

Mr. Rosington said, "My apologies, little lady," and, tail between his legs, took three large, hurried strides out of the room.
Nope, it wasn't his problem! Everybody else pretended not to
notice.

The Colonel was suddenly at my side—he moved stealthily
as if by nature—and murmured, "Baker, could I have a word?"

I looked at him to get a sense of what this meant. Was I fired
(already)? All my blunders of the evening ran through my head
like a highlight reel of a football game. *And late in the third
quarter, she fumbled the ice, causing a turnover. This has not been a
good night for Baker.*

The Colonel's demeanor was as apparently indifferent as it
had been when I had interviewed for the job that afternoon,
but his eyes carried a look of concern. Concern for me? I followed as he ambled in his long-legged way through a side door.

We ended up in what appeared to be a tearoom or something.

"Please close the door." I did. And braced myself.

He stood stock still, directly under a very bright baroque
chandelier. In his trim black suit, he had an almost regal appearance, especially among the Victorian chairs in bright floral
patterns, low, ornate antique-white tables, and, on the walls,
vaguely Impressionist paintings of women sitting or strolling
with parasols and lovely pastel gowns.

This was a feminine room. *Is the Colonel a widower?* I'd not
heard of nor seen any sign of a wife.

He nodded at me and turned to face the far wall, so I crossed
over to him.

"Baker," he said in his low, dry voice, "I'm afraid I must impose upon you a rather unpleasant task."

I wanted to say, *More unpleasant than serving rude, self-styled aristocrats?* but I restrained myself.

He pursed his lips, then pressed them together. "Henderson has managed to get himself a bit deep in his liquor," he said. "We must ask you to assist him."

"Assist him?"

"Yes, yes, Mrs. Henderson is having their chauffeur bring their car around to the garden entrance. I'd like you to lead him there."

I nodded, dreading having to deal with a drunken man.

The Colonel seemed to read my mind. "Henderson is one who appreciates beauty, Baker. A little charm, along with a firm grip, should help you manage."

"Is he sober enough to walk?"

"Ha, yes, a good question. Sober enough to walk? I believe so, with some assistance with his balance."

"Does he *want* to go?"

"Hmm, well, I understand that Mrs. Henderson has had a word with him on the matter, but he was, shall we say, reluctant."

So now I'm to bounce a drunk. Just great! "All right, so I get this guy out of the library and take him to the garden exit, where his wife is waiting with the car."

"You have the essence of it, Baker. I now return to the soirée. We will debrief later. I trust that you are enjoying yourself?"

A snort escaped before I could cut it off.

But he, without another word, turned away and ambled out of the room.

15

MR. HENDERSON, SPRAWLED ACROSS a chair in the corner of the library, drawled out words at a short, dark, sandy-haired gentleman I hadn't seen before.

I took what I hoped was a discreet route along the wall, and stopped twenty feet away. I looked around. Everybody was rapt in their own conversations—a window of opportunity. I approached Mr. Henderson with a most professional manner and bent to whisper in his ear, "Telephone call for you, Mr. Henderson."

He vaguely looked in my direction with bleary eyes. "Huh?" Then his eyes focused and he saw me, saw I was staff and presumably there on official business. "Telephone call?" He started patting his pockets. "Why didn't they just . . . Hmm. I lost my phone." He looked at me. "You dint find an iPhone? It's in a leather cover thing my daughter gave . . . Did you?"

"No, Mr. Henderson," I said. "They called on the landline."

"What—I wonder who knows I'm here? Who told them I'm

here?!" His face started getting red to match his eyes. "I have a fucking leak in my staff, Barney!"

A few people glanced over before returning to their parleys.

"If that's true," said sandy-haired Barney, "it's unfortunate."

"Damn right it's unfortunate!"

"Mr. Henderson," I said, and he spun on me, but his rallying moment of clarity seemed to fade.

"Who is it on—who . . . on the . . . phone?"

"I don't know, Mr. Henderson. If you'll come with me, it's just in the next room."

"Next room . . . huh . . ."

He slowly gathered himself and stood to his full six foot eight.

"Barney, it's the peasants," he slurred. "They just aren't what they used to be. No character. No inte—integrity. No steel in their souls. The peasants we have today"—he turned to me—"Nothing personal, sweetheart"—and then, to Barney, bellowed, "They're no good!"

He was getting hot. I needed to get him out quickly. "Mr. Henderson."

He squarely faced me. Even in stilettos I felt tiny next to him. He peered down at me and slurred in a low voice, "Ssso why don't you show me where this"—and he hiccupped—"phone is so I can t–talk to this person who doesn't know I'm here?"

Was that a joke? Good. This wasn't going to be so bad. I gave him a sweet, polite smile and led him to the nearest door. He turned with one last word for Barney. "We run a tight operation, Barney! Don't you . . ." and he trailed off, as if he lost the thread. I urged him through the door.

The sitting room through the door was dimly lit and empty.

Mr. Henderson asked with simple innocence, "Where's the phone?"

"Mr. Henderson, please remain calm."

"I'm calm!" He belched and teetered. "Are you" —burp—"calm?"

I put a steadying hand on his chest. "The Colonel asked me to assist you."

"The Colonel . . . ?"

"You've had a lot to drink—"

"Heh, damn right."

"—and so he asked me to help you."

"You're cute for a peasant girl. . . ." He scowled inward. "Oh, you people don't like that word. Not sup–supposed to use it" . . . he took a breath . . . "in front of you." He started rocking on his heels. I grabbed him by his lapels, for all the good it did, for he was going down no matter what I did.

Except he took a step back and caught himself—and I slammed into his belly.

"Sorry," he said. "Had a bit to drink—"

"You're shit-faced, Mr. Henderson."

That got his attention. He grinned at me. "No nonsense! Where'd the Colonel find you . . . ? I'm gonna hafta . . . ask . . ."

"This way, Mr. Henderson. Your wife is bringing your car around to the garden entrance."

His face turned sour. "My wife . . ." He belched again, then swallowed. "Uh," he moaned.

Shit! He was going to pop. I knew I had only seconds.

I grabbed his arm and towed him across the room to the far door. He staggered along with me, making unpleasant noises. I whipped the door open, revealing a brightly lit ornate corridor. Ms. Vitiello was walking by with a tray of teacups.

"Bathroom!" I panted.

She took us in with a glance, pirouetted gracefully, tray not making a sound, and pointed at a cream-white door.

Mr. Henderson let loose a wet burp. I pushed him into motion.

In seconds we were at the door.

I twisted the knob and shoved the door open, revealing that luxuriant marble washroom.

Mr. Henderson took two steps forward—his body convulsed—and a wet, chunky column of harlequin confetti sprayed from his mouth, covering everything within eight feet.

He lurched forward, sending the effluence all over the floor.

Momentarily stunned by the spectacular display, I recognized the shrimp cocktail hors d'oeuvres, the tomato bisque soup, and the medium-rare, dry-aged ribeye steak—but not the blueberries. *Where did he get blueberries?*

And then, in slow motion, he tottered over—and landed in the middle of the mess.

Which is where we came into this story. And so . . .

16

As Mr. Henderson's Bentley limousine rumbled away through the thickening snow, I, ass on ice, indulged in some I think very justified self-pity and colorful venting.

"Shit and fuck!"

"Language," said a woman's voice. Ms. d'Aleu stood in the doorway, all bundled up, briefcase in hand. "Are you all right?"

I tried to laugh with good spirit, but it came out more like an indignant cluck. "Been better."

"May I help?" She set down her briefcase and came out onto the drive to look at my leg. "Come on, let's get you patched up." Ms. d'Aleu put out her hand and pulled me back to my feet. Sore, cold, wet, tears of frustration freezing on my cheeks, but upright again, I put on my brave face and tried to ignore the throbbing in my knee. The skin felt raw. Ms. d'Aleu put her shoulder under my arm and helped me slide-shuffle back into the house.

As we made our way back along the marble promenade, my arms and back ached from muscling Mr. Henderson around. Ms. d'Aleu held my arm, steadying me, or else I might have flopped down right there and cried, *Leave me! Save yourself!* All I wanted at that point was to lie down.

She started to lead me toward the bathroom off the hall.

That bathroom.

"No," I said, "we don't want to go there!" My point was emphasized by a waft of vomitous odor. And a whiff of something else. Ammonia. Inside, someone wearing housekeeping's version of hazardous-waste gear was mopping the floor, cleaning up what was left of Mr. Henderson's gift for the evening.

"Come," Ms. d'Aleu said in a soothing voice. "We'll go to my suite."

Gently she drew me along, through a door leading away from the guests, into a backstage area with a freight elevator. It clanked and groaned its way upstairs, where she took me via a labyrinth of narrow corridors to another door that deposited us in the ornate hallway just outside of her office door. She pressed her palm against a touch plate. There was a soft beep and the door latch snicked.

She helped me inside.

In daytime, her office had been blindingly bright, and I was being blindingly dim, obsessed with my own neuroses, so I hadn't really noticed the décor. Now, lit with art deco sconces and a pair of Tiffany lamps, the space radiated warmth and comfort.

Ms. d'Aleu guided me to a burgundy-print *chaise longue*. Grasping the *méridienne*'s arm with one hand and Ms. d'Aleu's shoulder with the other, I slowly lowered myself onto the day-bed, my wounded leg extended. The stocking had a tear. I could see a bit of angry red skin through a small rent.

Ms. d'Aleu shrugged out of her overcoat, knelt down on the Persian rug, and slipped my shoe off. That alone brought relief. She brushed cold fingers along the rip in the hose and looked me in the eyes. "Let's get this off."

I reached toward my garter belt, but she stayed me with a hand. "Allow me," she said. Her eyes smiled.

I wasn't in any state to refuse some TLC, so I nodded okay and she gently reached up to unhook the straps and pull down the gossamer hose. Every now and then, her fingers touched my skin and a shiver ran up my back. I gasped—her hands were freezing. She whispered, "I'm sorry, my hands are cold." I would have said, *Cold hands, warm heart*, but my heart was skipping and I had to concentrate just to breathe.

She gently lifted the fabric to ease it past my abraded knee—which was oozing blood. Finally she slipped the soft stocking off of my foot.

She examined the wound. "Does it hurt?"

I shook my head, but my kneecap was pulsing at an increasing rate.

"Let's clean this up. Be right back." She rose and stepped quickly through a side door—to a private washroom, apparently. I heard a cabinet open.

While she rummaged around, I took some deep breaths to calm down, but all that accomplished was to invite my aching muscles to say hello. I told them to shut up, but they didn't listen.

A moment later she returned with a blue box. "I always keep some first-aid supplies handy." She gave me what almost seemed like a devious smile. "You never know, right?"

I could only nod.

She knelt in front of me. From the kit she produced some gauze and a brown bottle of peroxide, and gently dabbed the raw flesh. It felt like she was using battery acid, but I managed not to squeak. Next came a flesh-colored butterfly bandage. She smoothed it onto my knee.

"There you are."

"Thank you," I said.

She smiled. "Anytime." As she rose, she gave my thigh a quick squeeze. "Sit tight. I'll get you new stockings."

"Could I get a pair of the black opaque tights instead?"

She snorted. "Why so modest, Melody?"

I started, "Well—" but she stepped out of the office. The closed door gently behind her.

I settled back and gazed around the room.

Across from me stood a mahogany gun cabinet with interior lights showcasing a half-dozen rifles and shotguns—handy, I suppose, for whenever barbarians assaulted the castle.

On the adjacent wall hung framed photos of Ms. d'Aleu posing with all kinds of vanquished prey—geese, quail, rabbit, deer, a moose—and several human-silhouette targets with closely grouped holes in the head. I resolved never to get into a shoot-out with Ms. d'Aleu.

The door beeped, the latch snicked, and Ms. d'Aleu returned, eyes sparkling. "I know where they keep the uniform expendables. Got us a fresh pair." Standing there in her four-thousand-dollar suit, she opened the package and poured out into her hand stockings for my sexpot maid outfit. "These are the best quality," she said.

I reached for them, but she gave me a carnivorous look that made me a bit nervous. "You probably shouldn't bend your knee. Let me put these on for you."

Of course, that made logical sense.

She knelt down and rolled up one of the stockings in her hands. I extended my leg, and she slipped the soft material over my toes. You always have to be careful when drawing on stockings, especially if they're of fine quality, as these obviously were, but she seemed to slide them up my leg with extra attention and care. I think I might have enjoyed it, but I was too worked up—anxious about getting back on the job and worried what might happen if I stayed too long with her.

I had to lift my leg as she passed my knee, and then I started trembling a bit. Her icy hands were on either side of my leg. My heart was racing. I had to keep reminding myself to breathe. Briefly her finger on the inside touched high on my other thigh.

I jumped. *What presumably warm-blooded human has such frigid extremities?*

She smoothed the top hem of the stocking, untucking folds. Then she pointedly glanced at my hip and purred in a voice that was anything but frigid, "May I?"

I gave a little nod.

She slipped her hands up under my skirt and retrieved a strap from my garter belt, attaching it to the hose. When she reached for the back side, I rolled over onto my other hip to make the tab accessible, and she fastened that one, too.

A shiver ran through my entire body. The skin on my arms and legs tingled with goose bumps. And I was wet—a fact that mortified, embarrassed, thrilled, worried, delighted, shamed, and annoyed me, all in rapid succession. Could she tell?

She placed an arctic palm on my knee and said, "Your dress is a little damp."

Not trusting myself, I said, "Oh, I think it's fine."

She stood and gestured up with her hands. "Come on. I'll unbutton you."

That's exactly what I was afraid of.

I rose to my feet, turned around, and felt her work the unfastening process down my back. She slipped the dress off my shoulders and lowered it down. I stepped out of it, my back prickling.

To my relief and disappointment, she moved away from me, carrying the garment into the washroom. A blow dryer started up. A second later, there she was in the doorway, so professional in her pantsuit, holding high my skimpy little uniform while she waved the hot air back and forth across the material.

And there I was, standing there in the middle of her private office, clad in only my bra, panties, garter belt, and stockings, getting a chill from a draft somewhere—or maybe from remembered touches of her cold hands.

She smirked at me and said, "This will warm you up." She was enjoying this moment.

I said nothing, just shifted my weight and put a hand on my hip, as if to say, *I'm waiting*. A little id voice in my head added, *Come over here and ravish me like you mean it*. Then a bellow of superego outrage stepped in with *What are you thinking? She's technically your boss!* My ego came to a quite reasonable solution: *We don't want her to think we're easy.*

Ms. d'Aleu shut off the dryer and brought the dress back. I held my pose and raised an eyebrow, waiting. Well, she seemed to enjoy that ploy, too, for she smiled with her piercing eyes and squatted down, holding the dress open. I stepped into it. She drew it up—the warm fabric felt wonderful—and helped me slip my arms through the holes. Then she gently spun me around and set to buttoning up the back.

When she neared the top, she drew my hair free and draped it over my shoulder—and incidentally ran a light finger up my neck. More tingles. Three more buttons and then she drew my hair back. "All done," she whispered into my ear. I could smell the vanilla of shea butter.

I turned to face her. She stood close—our noses were mere inches apart. She lowered her eyes and ran her hands down from my ribs to my hips. "You could use a bit of tailoring." What? Did she want me to wear a bodycon dress?

I opened my mouth to protest—and she kissed me. It was the hottest kiss I've ever had from any girl—from anyone. It was soft and hard and cold and hot. I could smell her sweet skin. I wanted to melt around her.

Suddenly she stepped back, leaving me unsatiated. "There you are," she purred.

I shuddered a sigh, trying to calm myself.

"Maybe you need a moment," she said and moved to the door. *What?* "You're leaving *now*?"

"Take as long as you like," she said, "but they are probably looking for you downstairs."

Right. My job. *Cue bucket of cold water.*

She pulled the door open. "It will lock behind you." And then Ms. d'Aleu was gone. The door clicked shut.

I had no idea being a maid here could be so dangerous.

17

*W*ITH PROFESSIONAL PURPOSE, and having no idea how to find a hidden doorway to the backstage area, I marched down the hardwood corridor and clacked down three flights of the main marble staircase, arriving in the foyer, where the air was a bit chill from the front door's having been opened frequently in the past hour—a few guests had departed, apparently.

I crossed to the library, where I tried to inculcate within myself some kind of relief that things hadn't gone further upstairs, that I had escaped disaster and was now . . . safe.

As if.

I glanced down at my bandaged knee, visible through the sheer black fabric. *Yeah. Good as new!* I could still feel Ms. d'Aleu's fingers on my thighs. My back itched.

I glanced around. Mrs. Pegglesworth, looking a bit flushed but still poised, sat at a small table near the stair to the mezzanine with Ms. Wallis and Mrs. Beaulieu, while two men toward the back talked with their host about something appropriate only for lowered voices.

"Baker! Where's Mr. Henderson?" Mrs. Pegglesworth demanded.

I stood there with my mouth open, searching for something to say besides, *He puked up his bread pudding and passed out next to the toilet. The reckless fun here was too much for him and he fainted. He came on to the help and exposed himself as the weak lecher he is.*

I settled on, "Mr. and Mrs. Henderson departed some moments ago."

"How rude!" Mrs. Pegglesworth turned to her friends. "He was going to tell me about the outreach luncheon next week."

"I'm sure he'll get word to you," her companion, Mrs. Beaulieu, said. Mrs. Wallis nodded sagely.

Mrs. Pegglesworth sniffed. "He'll probably use that *email*! Whatever happened to the handwritten note?"

"Or engraved invitations," said Ms. Wallis. Mrs. Beaulieu stifled a giggle. Mrs. Pegglesworth glared at them.

I looked toward the back of the room; the Colonel was watching me. I offered a small smile while telepathically sending, *I got the drunken fool off without anybody seeing, no problem.* What I didn't send was, *And I got all hot and flustered when your beautiful lawyer almost seduced me!*

He gave the tiniest of nods and returned his attention to the gentlemen.

You're welcome.

"Baker!" cried Mrs. Pegglesworth, still fully lubricated. "If we're going to kick off the Colonel's campaign properly, we will need more martinis!"

The Colonel's campaign? Not Teddy Snoot's? The entire party shifted in my mind. This wasn't a cluster around the douchebag Teddy Snoot? *How did I miss that?*

Suddenly this entire affair took on a pathetic cast. How sad. Another billionaire wants to just waltz into politics and thinks he can win just by being rich. Was this someone I wanted to work for?

"Baker," Mrs. Pegglesworth said, "get your butt in motion or I'll have to put on your dress and show you how it's done!"

18

*N*OT UNTIL SOMETIME AFTER four in the morning did the remaining guests rise from their seats to depart for their lairs. Ten hours of drinking had rendered them rather intoxicated, albeit in that well-accustomed-to-it-by-now kind of way. And in ten hours of political talk, they had elevated themselves to the status of wise, insightful, proactive, daring, strong, and deserving—in fact, well deserving—keepers of the flame of the Republic. Each was comfortably intoxicated with both power and booze. Their contented eyes reflected elevated self-esteem and well-scrubbed consciences.

I, on the other hand, was stone-cold sober and yawning through clenched teeth. I'd been up for twenty-four hours. 4 a.m. was not only past my normal bedtime, it was close to my normal waking time. Left to my own predilections, I'm more of the early-to-bed, early-to-rise kind of girl—which is only natural when you have no social or dating life—whose idea of a great morning is sitting in the dark with a cup of French roast,

watching the first light of sunrise take gradual control of the
Manhattan skyline, not serving the world's finest liquors to an
entitled gaggle of dilettantes ineptly plotting political domi-
nation, starting with the candidacy of a billionaire who, they
clearly thought, was their puppet.

My feet were ready to cry mutiny. In fact my entire body
ached. I could hardly move. Therefore, during the departure
ceremony, Brick-house Betty here was quite content to maid
the cloakroom, fetching coats and hats, and handing them to
Ms. Metz, Mrs. Phillips, Ms. Odette, and Ms. Vitiello so they in
turn could perform the encloaking and behatting of everyone.

The guests, some with drinks still in hand, headed for their
limousines.

The last to take her leave was the Honorable Matilda
MacDougal-Oglethorpe, who was in a panic about her dog.
"Baby!" she called. "Baby!"

Mr. Haynes said, "She somehow jimmied the lock on the
kennel."

"Well if she's harmed," the Honorable Matilda MacDougal-
Oglethorpe snapped, "I'll see you up on charges!"

A couple of high-pitched yaps later, the little fuzzball trotted
into the foyer. I noted with alarm she had chunks of partially
digested blueberries embedded in the fur around her chops.
The Honorable Matilda MacDougal-Oglethorpe scooped her
up, cooed, "Did baby-wayby miss me?" and swept grandly out.

Mr. Haynes closed the front doors and latched them for the
night. He looked at us all. "A late evening. And a success, I believe. Leave the rest for the morning. Thank you." He bowed
his head.

We all thanked him back and drifted away.

As we walked down the backstage hallway—well, *they* walked; I *trudged*—Ms. Metz said, "What nice people they are."

The snickers of the others tipped me off to the sarcasm.

Mrs. Odette said, "At least it was an easy night."

An easy night?

I tagged along for the conversation as they started climbing a dimly lit, narrow staircase up three flights. Ms. Phillips began to quietly hum a languorous melody that tickled my memory.

Ms. Vitiello said, "I like it when they just sit around and drink."

"For a while there I was afraid they'd start dancing," said Ms. Odette.

Ms. Vitiello tipped her head to me. "When they dance, they drink twice as much."

"And stay past dawn."

Who knew being ridiculously rich required such stamina?

Ms. Phillips's tune quavered in agreement before resuming.

"And they spill things," said Ms. Odette.

"So what did you think of tonight?" asked Ms. Metz.

What did I think? My feet hurt. My back ached. My knee complained with every step. I shrugged my shoulders to work out the stiffness from muscling around Mr. Henderson and said, "It was interesting. I'm exhausted."

"You're out of shape."

"Says you," I said. Out of shape? *Why don't you try muscling Mr. Henderson out of the house and see how you feel!* "I'm not out of shape. I walk all over the city."

"Not in heels you don't, I'll bet."

She had me there.

"It's hard work for everyone," Ms. Vitiello said, but she didn't seem the least bit tired.

We finally reached the fourth floor—the floor that had the room I changed in. I wondered if my stuff was still there. Of course it was.

Ms. Metz waved good night as she strolled down a diverging hallway.

At a door marked the Artemis Room, Mrs. Odette said, *"Bonne nuit."*

Ms. Phillips paused her song to say good night at the Theia Room, and then resumed as she stepped inside.

A few steps farther and Ms. Vitiello said, "Welcome to service," before turning down a branching corridor.

With so many corridors and so many rooms, the castle seemed to be built to house a staff of fifty.

I stood alone at the intersection. The only sound was the faint rattle of a ventilator fan somewhere. The air smelled of incense and bleach.

Every bone and muscle in my body wanted to find the room I'd changed in—I was pretty sure it was just down the hall— and collapse on the bed. Or even better, go home and sleep in my own bed.

But the Colonel had said I'd get my money after everyone left. I had business downstairs.

19

*C*OME IN," said the Colonel.

I opened the door. Inside his small office (that, of course, also was considerably larger than my entire apartment), the Colonel, looking almost giddy, stood by a well-stocked bar.

"Baker, good evening. I'll be right with you. Please," and he gestured with a sweep of his arm, "sit."

Sitting sounded like a marvelous idea. I shuffled over to a comfy-looking armchair.

"Drink?" he asked.

That sounded like a *not* so marvelous idea—one shot was likely to knock me on my ass—but I said, "Sure," before my brain could stop my mouth.

As I sank into the deep cushions, he said, "Whenever I host a soirée, it takes me a while to wind down." *Wind down?* I was already completely unsprung. My feet throbbed, but I resisted the urge to kick off my shoes—I'd never have been able to get them on again.

A short-stemmed crystal snifter of caramel-colored liquor appeared in front of my nose.

Cognac! I accepted the glass, deciding that having a drink was in fact a wonderful idea.

The liquor smelled luscious—more exquisite than even the Courvoisier XO that Petra gave me when I had completed my dissertation. *That* had been a celebration. She and I drank the entire bottle over one long night, ordered in Chinese and pizza, and laughed and laughed over everything and nothing. I'd read hundreds of books and written scores of papers over the years, but handing in that epic document was the first time I felt like a scholar. When I confessed this to Petra, she had simply shrugged and said, as if the truth were obvious, "Of course you are scholar." Life had been clearer back then.

"Thank you for taking care of Henderson," the Colonel said.

"Oh, it was nothing," I said, ignoring my aching knee.

"Nevertheless . . ." He raised his glass in toast.

I took a sip of the cognac—which (I don't know how else to describe it) *blossomed* on my tongue, filling my mouth with vibrant colors.

"Croizet Cuvée Léonie," he said, beaming at my reaction. "I won't tell you how much I paid for it. It's rather embarrassing. In fact, there are people who would call for my hide if they knew we were drinking this. Well, they can stuff it! Silly bottle collectors! They don't realize that the real art is *inside* the bottle. You don't collect liquor. Collect paintings. Collect books. Collect stamps." He waggled his eyebrows. "*Drink* liquor."

I inhaled the delightful bouquet, thinking again of Petra. *What will she think of all this?*

The Colonel sank into the chair across from me, on the other side of a large oval ottoman. "He's not usually like that. Mr. Henderson. I wouldn't want anyone to get the wrong idea."

"Oh, I've seen drunk," I said. "All of your guests were drunk."

He laughed. "Yes, well, that, I'm afraid, is the familiar state of affairs with that crowd. What else?"

I didn't want to come across as rude, so I used my most polite voice to say, "Well . . . some people were obnoxious. Often arrogant." Okay, that was maybe a bit rude. But hey, they *were* obnoxious!

He just shrugged. "Right. Well, they are, aren't they? I'd say it comes with the money, but anybody can be a jerk. It doesn't require a portfolio."

What? No outrage? I wanted him to step up as the hero and demand to know who was obnoxious to me. Then I would tell him about Teddy's transgressions, and the Colonel would be outraged and, I don't know, have someone go egg his Ferrari.

But the Colonel was not interested in that. "What else?"

I wasn't about to describe my encounter with Ms. d'Aleu. She was beside the point. Now was my chance to impress the Colonel with my sharp mind, my astute observations, and my broad knowledge of all—well, many—things political. (You don't grow up a Congressman's daughter without absorbing *some* bits of political pith.) I decided to dive right in. "You're running for the Senate."

His eyebrows lifted and creased. "You caught that, did you?"

"Kind of hard to miss."

He nodded. This was the conversation he sought. "And what do you think?"

"Your guests' enthusiasm is obvious."

He seemed pleased to hear that. "Yes, yes, yes, they're good people."

I wouldn't have gone *that* far, but they were *his* friends, not mine. "They love that you're running. It was practically the only thing anyone talked about."

"Ah," he said, and for a moment he just nodded with an inward, toothy grin, obviously pleased with the whole thing. That's the way with dilettantes, though, isn't it? They're so proud of themselves for daring to dabble. He had no idea what he was getting himself into. I saw that with my father's election campaigns. The Colonel would get ripped off and eaten up.

Well, that was his business. Getting me off this maiding duty as soon as possible and into some proper research work was mine.

The Colonel put his long feet up on the ottoman between us; he wore these odd black silk socks with bright red patches on his toes and heels. I kept my nose tucked into my glass.

"Tell me more," he said, "about this enthusiasm you mentioned."

I took another sip of the cognac and let the sensory indulgence speak to me. "Some of the guests," I said, "seemed enthusiastic about *you* as a candidate."

"Only some?"

"Mr. Henderson, for example."

"Ah, yes." He rubbed his chin. "Anyone else?"

I had to mull over how to break it to him. I finally said, "I was watching to see what people's attitudes were, but I'm not sure anyone else voiced enthusiasm about you so much as enthusiasm for what they could do once they were in power. What they would get."

The Colonel leaned forward, a bit surprised and very interested. "Tell me more, Baker."

"Well, Mr. Henderson was different. He asked me"—and I visualized the scene to hear his words—"'Would you rather vote for an extremist, hypocritical son of a bitch or an upstanding, dignified man of breeding?'"

"Ha!" the Colonel chortled. "And what did you say?"

"I asked whether either told the truth."

He slapped his knee. "Ha!"

I went for another sip, but my glass was empty.

"More cognac?"

"Please."

He accepted my glass and went to the bar. "I haven't received any performance reviews from Haynes or Metz, but I think the guests found you to be quite convincing," he said as the decanter tinked against the snifter. "You're a natural, Baker."

"I'm glad I could help in a pinch," I said.

He stood over me, holding both drinks. "It has me thinking. We may have stumbled across the perfect situation."

"You have?" I asked.

"The two of us. You and I." His silly grin was making me uneasy. What was he thinking?

"How do I fit into it?" I asked.

The cognac sloshed in the snifters as he gestured with excitement. "You're an average American—well, except for being smart and educated. But you're not of my class—my class is a bunch of self-important prigs, if you ask me, but that's neither

here nor there—and yet you're not of the servant class, either."
He chuckled—no, he chortled. "That's precisely it," he almost shouted. "You're so bourgeois, you don't fit in here." He
grinned, showing all of his teeth. "Which is why you're perfect!"

"Perfect? For what?"

He finally handed me the cognac, and said with delight, "To
remain our new maid through the entire campaign! Through
November at least. Maybe beyond that."

What?

I quaffed the full double shot of cognac right down. My
throat closed up, burning coursed through my chest, and a
floral tingle filled my sinuses.

He smiled, took my empty glass, and went back to the bar.

"Look," he said, "I'm always the last to know about anything. Nobody tells the boss anything. I see only the top-level
surface, the finished sausage, so to speak. The meat grinder
mashing up all the gristle and bone and cartilage"—lovely im-
agery, yes?—"is beyond my purview. Baker, I need you to be
there when the sausage is being made, tell me what they're
putting into it, if any of the ingredients are rotten or likely to
give me indigestion."

He handed me a refilled cognac. I took a gulp to wash away
that metaphor, and cautiously asked him, "So what are you asking me to do, exactly?"

"Find out whom I can trust. My campaign headquarters will
be right here in this house. As a maid of the house, you will have
free and full access to the campaign staff, campaign meetings,
everything happening in my entire campaign. You watch and
listen, and at the end of each day, we debrief here, you give me

an honest, educated, middle-class assessment of what's happening, including what's happening behind my back."

I can tell you, at that point I was feeling just a bit outraged. I'd come all the way up here to apply for a research position, and in a moment of compassion or opportunism or foolishness, I volunteered to help him out of a jam. And this is what I get? "You want me to be a maid and your spy?" *Are you fucking kidding me?*

"You have the essence of it. As our new maid, you will be my eyes and ears. A fly on the wall. A secret agent, if you will." He grinned at that.

I asked, dripping with sarcasm, "Do I get a pistol to strap to my thigh?"

He waved that off. "No need. We'll have a full security detail."

Including Ms. d'Aleu, I thought to myself.

"You, Baker, will just play the part. Blend in. And observe. Oh, you'll be terrific, I'm sure."

My head was swimming. I took another swallow of cognac.

He cocked his head. "I assume it presents no trouble for you to stay here on the estate from time to time, as your duties demand."

Stay here? As in live here? Was this a good thing or a bad thing? Would working here suck up all my time? Or would I have opportunity to write?

As if he'd heard my thoughts, he added, "You'll have your own room. With the long hours, you may find it convenient."

He extended his hand to shake.

I looked at it. Was I really up to doing this? "I would still need to go to the city to get some things."

"Fine. Fine."

I let out a big, deep, existential sigh. "I can't think. I'm exhausted."

"Being a maid is hard work, is it?" he asked, apparently genuinely curious.

Had he never paid attention? "Whatever you're paying them," I said, "it's not nearly enough."

"That's a thought. Tomorrow I'll have Haynes double everyone's salary. Speaking of pay."

He withdrew his hand, reached into his jacket pocket, and produced a fat envelope. He handed it to me.

I peeked inside—a fat stack of $100 bills.

He put out his hand again.

I hesitated.

"Oh, come on," he said. "This is going to be fun!"

Fun? Fun?

I let my fingers glide over the tops of the crisp one-hundred-dollar bills.

The story continues in
The Candidate's Maid, Book Two:
The Colonel's Secret Service

ACKNOWLEDGMENTS

This book began years ago as a single paragraph that then sat in the metaphorical drawer until I didn't remember writing it anymore. A couple of years ago, as our politics entered a new phase, I dusted it off and wrote a complete novel. Unfortunately, or fortunately, after I set the manuscript aside to get some distance, the politics of this country continued to evolve, rapidly outstripping even the most outrageous and over-the-top satire I had in that draft. This book is a reboot.

Without my editor and best friend, Katherine M. Lawrence, this book would not exist at all. Her criticism, insightful editing, instincts, and unrelenting dedication have helped me persevere through this process.

Gratitude goes to Tiffany Yates Martin, FoxPrint Editorial, for her editorial work on an early draft.

Greatly valued with my appreciation are Tonia Hurst, whose feedback I value highly, and my regular crit readers, Leslie Smith and Paige Danes, who manage to check my literary insanity every couple of weeks.

Special and heartfelt thanks go to readers Crystal Thieringer, Roslynn Pryor, Janet Brantley, and Carolyn Studer for their sharp and timely feedback as I was blasting out that first draft.

Finally, I would not be writing fictional tales were it not for the steady and unwavering encouragement, support, and love from my mother, whose critical mind and poetic soul are constant inspirations, my sister, whose strength and tenacity humbles me, my beautiful niece, who at fifteen years old is outpacing everything I've done, and my late father, who always wanted the best for me and never let me forget my creative endeavors. Love you all!

—*LLS, Boulder*

ABOUT THE AUTHOR

Over the years, Laura Lis Scott has (yes) waited tables, delivered campus mail, driven a truck (more like a van), wordprocessed business and legal documents, written and produced videos, produced B-movie trailers, directed television, designed and developed websites, edited magazine articles, created logos, blogged amateurly (often amateurishly) and professionally, co-founded a few companies, raced cars (on actual racetracks—street racing is dumb), and written a handful of stories.

When she's not writing her own stuff, Laura serves as the editor for Katherine M. Lawrence's Yamabuki novels set in 12th-century Japan.

Laura has BA from The University of Chicago and an MFA from Columbia University of New York. Alas, she has no PhD; she hopes you'll forgive her for that. She lives in Colorado, where the sun always shines, even on the cloudy days.

The Candidate's Maid is her first novel. Before that, she just shouted at the television.

Laura's links:

¶ website: LauraLisScott.com

¶ Facebook: www.facebook.com/lauralisscott

¶ Twitter: @lauralisscott

¶ Subscribe to Laura's newsletter at eepurl.com/NyRDb

Excerpt from

The Candidate's Maid, Book Two:
The Colonel's Secret Service

*T*HE *POP POP POP* of gunfire could be heard even in the backstage innards of the castle. Like many others, I found myself leaving my duties to peer out the library window at Mr. Henderson, who was working a pump-action shotgun, trying to take down some airborne nemesis high overhead, out of our field of view. *Pop!* Pump. *Pop!* "Come closer, you bastards!"

"Everybody down!" One of the security giants bounded in on feet lighter than should have been possible, and took a position against the wall next to the window, assault rifle ready.

"It's just Mr. Henderson," I said.

"Down!"

I squatted down. "He's shooting some birds, I think."

"Quiet!" His pasty white face flushed pink. "Colonel, are you okay?"

Half-bent over at the far end of the room by the stacks, the Colonel nodded. "Fine."

The giant touched the headset stuck in his ear. "Porkchop in the library. Diamond and one trinket secure."

Trinket? I'm a trinket?

He listened for a moment, then snapped his head in front of the window to get a look.

"10-14," he said. "Single intruder with pump shotgun. Twenty, exterior front drive."

Two more of Sparky's team moved silently past the doorway to the foyer, approaching toward the front entrance. I heard the front door open. Shouting. "Down! On the floor!"

Mr. Henderson's voice shouted, "God damn it!"

Then there were sounds of a physical tussle. Porkchop leveled his weapon at the open doorway to the foyer. There were some thumps and clatters. Moments later, Mr. Henderson, shotgun cradled in his arm, marched into the library—

"Freeze!" shouted Porkchop.

Mr. Henderson didn't flinch. "Will you guys settle down?"

"It's all right," said the Colonel. "He's a friend."

Porkchop held a moment, then straightened, bringing is rifle to his chest.

Mr. Henderson chuckled. "You guys are trying, I'll give you that."

From the foyer, the two hulking security men entered slowly. The freckled redhead, whose head barely cleared the doorjamb, was rubbing his neck. The dark-skinned Samoan, who looked to be even bigger, rolled his shoulder.

Ignoring them, Mr. Henderson squatted down by the doors and started digging in a bag. "They flew out of range."

"Ducks?" asked Porkchop. Mr. Henderson didn't answer.

Sparky stepped into the library and planted himself, legs wide, arms folded. "Planning any more hunting?"

Mr. Henderson dug a bread loaf-sized box out. "I'm gonna give 'em a few. Let 'em think they beat me, and try again."

He flipped open the top, revealing neat rows of red three-inch shells, and inserted one into the side of the gun.

"Double-aught buck didn't get the point across. We'll see how they like a Tri-Ball welcome."

He turned the gun upside-down and continued loading, his eyes following with purpose each shell as it moved from box to the gun, slipping into the carrier.

"Stand down for the moment," Sparky said. "Pinball, Molly, check the perimeter. Porkchop, secure the rear."

The three security men lumbered out.

Finished with his loading, Mr. Henderson stood, sweaty brow over an expression of grim satisfaction. "Those buzzards won't know what hit them. Or maybe they will, and I'll be on the news. Any of those drones come close to within range, let me know."

"*We're* supposed to be the only ones shooting firearms on the premises."

"Yeah, well, change in plans, Sparky. I'm not gonna have CNN peeping in our windows like a bunch of perverts. This is private property!" Mr. Henderson took a position by the window and peered out at the sky.

Sparky left to his unseen world of seeing everything.

The Colonel took a seat and read a book. I stood to the side, waiting to be needed.

It was about twenty minutes later when Mr. Henderson moved like lightning out the door.

Pop! "Come on!" he shouted. *Pop!* "Ha!"

The Colonel and I looked at each other, waiting. This time the security detail remained out of sight.

A minute later, Mr. Henderson entered the library with prey in hand—a large, half-shattered spider-shaped octocopter drone—and set it on an empty library table.

The Colonel and I joined him to peer at it up close. It looked like a giant flying spider, broken into a few pieces.

"They were on the west side, just outside the third-floor windows."

The Colonel slipped on his readers. "The camera seems to be intact."

"I'll take care of that," Mr. Henderson said, grasping the piece with a thick hand and snapping it off of the center mount of the damaged drone.

"Give it to me," the Colonel said.

Mr. Henderson's face fell, but he handed it over.

The Colonel peered at it, then held it out at arm's length, pointed at his face.

"One of the very important issues our nation faces," he said in a clear voice, "is the loss of privacy."

He continued talking, but Cale Plumout and Tatiana Willoughby arrived just then and I had to go help them with their coats.

Just as the three of us entered the library, the Colonel slammed his hand holding the camera, lens down, against the hardwood table.

Released from his grip, the camera settled onto the table in six or seven pieces of plastic and glass.

Mr. Henderson beamed at him.

Cale's entire face lit up like it was Christmas. "Whoa! A Droidworx SkyJib-8 Titanium!" He rushed to the table and saw the degree of damage to the drone. "Dude, you crash it?"

Tatiana, meanwhile, had her nose close to her phone. "Found it." She went into the sitting room—now the makeshift campaign media center—and turned on the 98-inch 8K LED screen. Several campaign staffers crowded around.

I lingered along the wall and watched.

Tatiana tapped on her phone. A video feed launched on screen:

The shot was from high up, flying over the estate. Even from a thousand feet up, the castle looked huge.

"Our Hot Witness Eagle Eye camera," said the glib voice of online news anchor sensation Rex Rexer, "got close to the Colonel's estimated half-billion-dollar compound to try to verify rumors that some of the biggest players among the rich and powerful were meeting with the Colonel."

The view flew down closer and zoomed in on the windows, looking in through each one.

"While merely doing our best to serve the public interest and our right to know what our elected officials, both elected and aspiring, are really up to, we were met by the Colonel's staff by violence."

The image panned and tilted down to see Mr. Henderson far below, in front of the portico, aiming a shotgun at the camera—

—The picture glitched, and the picture started spinning.

The screen cut to Rex Rexer in his trademark black t-shirt and mussed hair. "That was almost cool," he said. "Check this."

And the screen cut back to the video, this time inside the

Colonel's library. The shaky image turned up to wide angle close-up of the Colonel. He said, "We will be filing charges with the appropriate authorities. I mean the invasion of personal privacy by the government, without probable cause, without oversight, without checks and balances. This is a topic I shall raise during this campaign."

The picture spun. We saw a flash of the chandelier overhead, and the picture went dark.

"That rocks," said Tatiana.

The screen cut back to Rex Rexer grinning ear to ear. "Dude!"

At that, several staffers busted out in laughter, high-fiving each other.

But Ms. Thorndike was not pleased and passed a sour gaze across all of them, eventually landing on me across the room.

I wiped the smile off of my face and made my exit. No, I wasn't running away. I didn't answer to her.

I didn't.

THE CANDIDATE'S MAID, BOOK TWO:
THE COLONEL'S SECRET SERVICE
WILL BE RELEASED MAY 2016

ABOUT TOOT SWEET INK

Toot Sweet Ink is an imprint of Toot Sweet Inc., an independent publisher based in Boulder, Colorado.

Watch for our upcoming releases in science fiction, non-fiction, women's contemporary fiction, humor, and historical fiction, including the series of samurai novels by Katherine M. Lawrence, which follow the adventures of Yamabuki, a woman warrior in 12th-century Japan.

Twitter: @TootSweetInk

Facebook: www.facebook.com/tootsweetink

Website: TootSweet.ink

Newsletter: Get updates and learn about new releases and discount opportunities on our upcoming titles by signing up at eepurl.com/K8XVn